MW00438494

That, at least, was reassuring. Damon was quite close to the man now. At his feet was a large, wolfish animal, lounging in a relaxed manner but with head up, ears erect, and eyes interestedly forward. The man spoke. "This is Kira. My name is Harrod Dan, a person of this planet. One of roughly thirty thousand."

Damon looked puzzled. "On the whole planet?" Harrod seemed amused at the question.

"That's the whole planet. We arrived at our present population purposefully and for a good reason. This world as you now see it is its embodiment." Damon looked around him at the vaulted splendor of the library and the greater splendor beyond it and marveled at this race that appeared so at peace with itself and with the animal world as well. Damon shook his head groggily.

Harrod Dan smiled. "There's more to the solution. I've already introduced you to Kira Sor. Let me do so again."

THE MAN HELD A BOOK.

JOEL RICHARDS

PINDHAREE

A TOM DOHERTY ASSOCIATES BOOK

This is a work of fiction. All the characters and events portrayed in this book are fictional, and any resemblance to real people or incidents is purely coincidental.

PINDHAREE

Copyright © 1986 by Joel Richards

All rights reserved, including the right to reproduce this book or portions thereof in any form.

Excerpt p. 211 from Edmund Keeley and Philip Sherrard, trans. *C. P. Cavafy: Collected Poems*, ed. George Savidis. Translation copyright © 1975 by Edmund Keeley and Philip Sherrard. Reprinted by permission of the Princeton University Press.

First printing: July 1986

A TOR Book

Published by Tom Doherty Associates
49 West 24 Street
New York, N.Y. 10010

Cover art by David Mattingly

ISBN: 0-812-55141-9
CAN. ED.: 0-812-55142-7

Printed in the United States

0 9 8 7 6 5 4 3 2 1

For Jytte, who understands loyalty—
and other qualities higher on the value scale.

Part I

LEAVING ─────────

There was a stench of burnt flesh in the heavy air. Some of it was human.

It didn't take sophisticated weaponry to produce that smell. Man had known it since his primitive origins.

The Captain was stalking the charnel field, picking his way through the fused metal of the Cygnan land tracker, the scattered fragments of chitinous shell, an occasional jointed limb forcibly disjointed from its arthropod body. And the softer, fleshy charred remains of human corpses.

Some of the remains were recognizable. Commander Harding, Damon's department head, was one. He had been more a man of science than a military man, but he had worn a uniform—one that smoldered now, melding its stench with his.

Everyone kept out of the Captain's seething passage through the mess. Major Khan was kneeling by the dead form of Lieutenant de Genova, his face expressionless. Khan talked seldom, not at all now. The Exec stood well to the side, his heat burns being treated by the ship's doctor, his face defiant. As the doctor dabbed at his burns the Exec eyed the party of Cygnans warily. They, too, stood aloof, their eye-stalks roving over the scene, perhaps picking out an exploded fragment in recognition.

The Captain raised his gaze from ground level and strode toward Damon, his long legs eating up the space between them. Damon stiffened to attention.

"As you were, Mr. Hart," the Captain said tightly. "Have you spoken with the Cygnans?"

"Yes, sir. They've had outside contact before, though not with humans. They speak Sector Basic."

"What's their version?"

Damon took a breath. "Not surprisingly, Captain, they find our body types alien. Reading between the lines, repulsive. Like any race believing themselves broad-minded, they tried to rise above surface impressions, to know us better and to grasp our culture. The Exec suggested that this might best be achieved through a Terran colony here."

A disciplined man, the Captain said nothing, but his next intake of breath was a controlled hiss. Damon paused, but the Captain eyed him steadily, his stare urging him to continue.

"This suggestion shocked—or disgusted—the Cygnans as a group. A couple of them involuntarily let their limbs approach their weapons. They admit to that and apologize. The Exec went further. He drew his side arm and fired."

"I see," the Captain said. He beckoned to his orderly, who was standing discreetly out of earshot. The man approached. "Ask Major Khan and Commander Bering to come here."

The Captain addressed himself to the Exec first.

"The Cygnans confirm your statement that they reached for their weapons. Involuntarily, they state, in reaction to your proposal to colonize. You said nothing of this when you stated the case before."

"The crabs went for their guns, Captain," the Exec maintained, ignoring the rebuke. "I acted as I thought the situation warranted."

"You fired yours. They didn't. Until after. Damn it, this isn't a fast draw contest!"

The Exec glowered but held silence.

The Captain turned to Khan, a trim, brown-skinned figure in marine khakis. Khan's eyes glittered blackly and his cheekbones seemed to have hardened beyond Damon's recollection of his face.

"Major Khan," the Captain rapped out, "you shall personally accompany all contact parties here and on any other worlds we may visit. Mr. Hart is now acting department head of Alien Contact. You will instruct your marines to fire their weapons only on express command from myself, you, or Mr. Hart. None other. Is that clear?''

"Yes, sir.''

The Captain turned his gaze to the Exec. ''And clear to you, Commander?''

The Exec's face was red, from flash burns or suppressed feelings. He nodded and, when the Captain continued his piercing gaze, bit out, ''Yes.''

"You're dismissed. Major Khan, I'd like to see you in my quarters at 1800 hours. Mr. Hart, please remain.''

Damon and the Captain stood together in silence as the marine major and the Exec withdrew, looking beyond their figures, looking beyond the meeting place of two races to the rolling green hills in the distance, to the beaches and the clear lagoons where the Cygnans made their wicker cities, half in the water, half on the shimmering sand that met it. The Captain turned to Damon.

"Commander Harding was a friend. You're an inexperienced and unknown quantity to me, but he thought a good deal of your abilities. You're going to use them and I'm going to use them. I have to. In particular, I want you free to act on your judgment on matters of alien contact. Your orders outrank all others, save mine. You know that now, Major Khan does, and so does Commander Bering.'' He paused.

'You won't have to rub his nose in it. Whatever his limitations, don't take the Executive Officer for a fool. He's not one.''

The Captain turned away, ending the interview, and strode toward his gig. His orderly fell in behind.

Damon turned for a last look at the scorched field amidst the lush greenery. It wasn't a battlefield, only a skirmish field, but it was a lasting reminder till the grass grew over it—maybe longer—of a fearsome barrier between mankind and an intelligent race that had the misfortune to resemble the monsters of the Exec's boyhood closet.

The gig had lifted now, taking the Captain back to the ship where he had safely been, as Navy regs demanded when initial contact had been made. His subordinates had acted, and he would pay a personal price. This field was also the burying ground of the Captain's chances for advancement.

Damon had seen enough. He walked toward the scout. It was time to leave. There were other worlds to visit.

Kira loped down the narrow forest pathway, a three-quarter speed pace that she could sustain indefinitely. The dirt path, overlaid with pine needles, twisted and turned around fallen logs and outjutting boulders. Their proximity gave her an illusion of speed as they flashed by, some grazing her lean flanks. Beside her the stream raced its parallel course.

Occasionally she would dart off the trail, picking her way through the tangles of brush and sword fern to lap a mouthful of cold water.

There was a mild urgency to Kira's passage, but no headlong haste. She ran because she chose to. Curiosity and exuberance drove her to stretch her body and her stride.

This was not a blind tear through the woods. Miles downstream the current broadened from its steep rocky course and flowed more placidly through a broad grass meadowland. There would be no tangle of overhead foliage to screen the sun. It would be too hot for running. Too dangerous, as well. There was something there that demanded a cautious approach.

Her stride closed as she topped a small rise in the trail. Below her was a deep rock pool, fed by a cascade of water down a moss-slick rock slide. She could see the shadowed forms where the high sun hit the water, and she sent a questing probe ahead. A couple of low order feral pings bounced back, rapaciousness mixed with fear. A flick or two of tail fins, and the shadows had scuttered between sheltering rocks. The largest shape moved not at all, facing upstream near the base of the cataract. Kira's ping triggered a level one greeting and dismissal, a surface veneer of enveloping, gloss-hard, spherical sheen around the Thinker's essence.

Kira stopped and looked down. Her sides were heaving. She had blown her undercoat some weeks before; still her mouth lolled open as she dissipated heat. Feeling venturesome, she risked a follow-up in the override mode. An iron tang of adrenaline surrounded the message core: *alien presence.*

There was no telling whether a Thinker would respond to that. Usually they had put aside emotional susceptibilities, yet the message content, even stripped of its emotionalism, might arouse interest. It depended on how deep the Thinker was working, whether the subject was along his main line of inquiry.

A moment passed, and Kira felt a heavy presence rush in around her: underlying sense impressions of cold, clear, oxygenated water; a tilting vision plane of refracted light and prisms as the scaly body rolled, and a broad level interrogatory.

Spaceship in the meadow, Kira pinged. *What is your interest?*

Kira felt a ping laden with a sense of void, nothingness deep and black. A pinpoint of light appeared, attempted resolution, then suffused to blurriness. *Ontology. Being and reality. If they seek along those lines, convey my interest.*

Kira affirmed, then felt again the shiny billiard-ball shield of dismissal. She turned down the trail.

Her pace slackened as the terrain leveled. When she reached the border of the woods her breathing was normal and her heartbeat steady. She peered out through savannah grass.

There it was—a silver taper on its side, its bulk

mashing grassland and grooving soil. Bubbles studded the hull. Weapon pods, most likely. There was no motion or activity. They were probably running life-support tests.

A shadow swept swiftly along the ground. She felt an overhead presence and looked up. Gliding and banking above, wings outstretched and motionless, was a raptor. One Kira did not know. Through overtones of *domain* and *freedom* Kira sensed the shadow of other minds beyond.

Both Kira and the raptor adopted the safer passive mode. They could sense a distant gabble of checklisted preparations being carried out within the ship. They dared not try for visual resolution and risk triggering a premature response.

They waited. At length a broad entry port slid open and a ramp extended. Figures appeared at the companionway.

Humans! Kira felt disappointment.

They do not pick us up. Kira felt the raptor's talons extend, curling down, and his shoulders stoop. She could sense him risking a light probe, the lightest prick of his mind's talons. She followed his slant and received a low level reading of atmospheric testing laconically being carried out. The subject did not note their foray.

Not a good beginning, the raptor hazarded sourly. *A warship. Humans. Not overly advanced, it seems. Lucky, under the circumstances.*

Still, we must deal with them, Kira responded.

They are here, the raptor agreed. *For the moment.*

There were not many men on this world. Harrod Dan received Kira's report and the Council's call while in his fields. He wiped his forehead, feeling the salty sweat trickle through his eyebrows into his eyes. Fieldwork was an uncommon activity among the Once Born. He had chosen to do it. It fitted his present state of development. It was satisfying and had its rewards. An unexpected one—if such it could be called—loomed ahead.

It would cost harder work than in the fields.

"Don't make the mistake of considering the Exec stupid," Khan said evenly as he advanced his king's bishop. "Coarse manners and intelligence are not mutually exclusive. Xenophobia either."

"The Captain said the same. Everyone seems to think me naive enough to think the Exec stupid. I gather that you consider him more dangerous than he looks."

"He is, particularly considering who pushes his buttons."

Damon looked up sharply at the marine major, who continued in the same equable tones. "He blunts his own intelligence, of course. Intemperance overrules it. Prejudice blinds it. He is incapable of objectively evaluating alien cultures, or even me, for instance. If he were a certain type of Britisher, he'd consider me a wog, useful for keeping other wogs in line. Doubtless there's some North American equivalent.''

Damon studied the board while digesting these seeming indiscretions and wondering what motivated them. Rachman Khan Pindharee, commandant of the marine detachment, had always seemed a straightforward soldier, aloof and reserved.

''Whose tool is he, Rachman?''

''There is a certain irony here, of course,'' continued Khan on his own tangent, ''in that the policies of the Executive Officer's 'constituency,' shall we say, and that of my state are the same. No matter that there are different reasons. My state's lie in seeking an outlet for surplus—shall we say disruptive?—population. His political backers seek commercial aggrandizement.''

''The same net result,'' observed Damon dourly. ''Colonize wherever possible. In other words, wherever a native culture appears even slightly less technologically advanced than ours. Has it occurred to you, Rachman, how little we've developed morally over the centuries?''

Khan laughed shortly, and advanced a knight. ''A commonplace observation. To any thinking man, at least. Of course, I don't mean this bunch.'' He indicated with a slight nod of his head the groups of officers intent on their wardroom card and billiard games. ''Centurions all. Which proves your point, but such a self-obvious one that it hardly needs proving anew.''

"I wasn't trying to be profound, Rachman. Merely pointing out that for all our recognition of it, the problem still remains, and in rather immediate form.''

"Which is why we're having a game of chess, and I'm talking freely, if a bit obliquely, of dangerous matters. Like subordinating political directives to acting decently in our outworld relations.''

Damon continued his narrow regard of Khan. "Are these the Captain's views as well? We're *supposed* to be nonpolitical, I'd heard.''

Khan smiled thinly. "I hope that you have no illusions about the Captain. He has few if any about himself. He may well be the only true nonpolitical senior officer on this ship—for all the propaganda about the Navy's divorce from politics—but that's only because no one political faction would tolerate another's man as Captain. By the time we get home, neither I nor the Captain—nor the Exec—expect this to be so. The Exec's faction, allied with the overpopulated states, will be in control.''

"You seem remarkably well informed, Rachman. Tell me this—why doesn't the Captain simply relieve the Exec? He's got the guns—the Exec's behavior in Cygnus.''

"Because the Exec relieved is a bigger menace. He'd have nothing further to lose. He'd be continually plotting and eventually acting.''

"Do you mean mutiny? Come on, Rachman!"

"Try it under a different name. Perhaps he'd have the Captain's food juiced, then relieve him for irregular and irresponsible behavior. Incapacity for command."

"I don't believe it. It's too Byzantine for words."

"Don't be so sure. There are bigger stakes here than a Byzantine empire. And remember that the doctor's the Exec's man. Or, rather, they're both someone else's men, and that someone else is likely to be in power when we get home."

"Including your government, I gather."

"Perhaps. But my loyalties aren't narrow or blind or bought. And those of my government and myself stop far short of genocide. We've known that too well at home."

The city was large but not sprawling. On the contrary, it stretched upward, supported on six huge pillars, themselves hollowed with lift shafts in their cores and faced with a beehive of living units and office quarters. The bulk of the city based out several thousand feet from ground level, in multifaceted tiers and terraces, irregular and staggered in arrangement. There was no readily grasped layout to the vast complex. Lift shafts and moving and stationary ramps connected shopping areas, parks, living clusters, office concentrations in what seemed to be haphazard order. Perhaps that had made life more interesting to the inhabitants, if more puzzling to visitors unfamiliar with the language or planning rationale.

The city was immense. Its skyward reach and the scale of its surroundings made it seem not so. It towered by the shore of a forested lake, which was perhaps forty miles long by ten wide. At the city's back and in all other directions, great woods and rolling hills ranged for miles beyond sight, dwarfing even the city's bulk. Some tens of millions of inhabitants had lived, worked, played, within the city's massive yet graceful confine. Beyond that confine lay a habitat untouched, or perhaps reclaimed. Highways, factories, refuse heaps—who knew what suburban scars the green covered up?

There was no one to ask. Once there had been humans. The city's artworks and artifacts, commercial displays, sculptures spoke to that. Now the city knew activity but no life. Power was there at a touch. Moving ramps, lifts, lights worked when activated by human presence. Cleaning mechanisms policed a city that no one littered.

There was life on the planet. It teemed with it, vital and prolific. But the city was empty and intelligent life seemed nonexistent.

In the end the city's immensity defeated them. There were cubic miles to be explored and no guide to assist them. Long traverses and forays produced repetition but little knowledge. They had too few social scientists to do it well. The natural scientists and the technicians were cataloguing the remainder of the planet with a view to man's uses of it were its natural heirs not to be found. Perhaps even if they were.

Damon was a professional at alien contact. Its appeal lay in counterbalancing the exotic and the reward of discovery with a potential for danger. It was the ultimate adventure.

But not without its rules. One prime dictum dominated: Approach the contact from a distance. Allow him to assess and reassess the situation at his pace.

Damon looked up from his campfire to the light streaming across the lake from a tower of the abandoned city. It had not been there a moment before. Not much more than a pinpoint, the light fanned to a shimmering line on the lake's surface. Damon had met another professional.

He worked to restrain his impatience. A ferric tang of adrenaline pumped in his nostrils with every breath, tingeing the coffee aroma from the cup he now gripped with both hands. He took another sip and waited till his mind had wrested control from his emotions. Then he strode to the water's edge and dipped out a pot of water, sending a school of minnowlike fish scuttling. He threw it on the fire and kicked the ashes. Briskly he assembled his gear and threw it back into the skimmer. A part of him regretted leaving his carefully laid bed of conifer needles, but then he had already had the cool dusk swim, the fire-cooked dinner.

Damon put the skimmer on air cushion and started across the lake. The craft was virtually soundless. A small moon had risen from behind the city's towering bulk, its pale aura sufficing for cross-lake navigation. Nonetheless he switched on the skimmer's running lights. An answering gesture of open hands.

As he neared the city he hit the control, raising the craft off its air cushion, and started upward.

The light came from the head of one of the glassed-tower bulwarks, lancing out from an interior source across a park-lined landing stage. The landing platform was smaller in scale than the mass approaches at the city's commercial core, and the surrounding landscaping seemed more placidly laid out, less openly functional in traffic control. Small paths wandered from the main approachways. Viewed from his hovering skimmer, they made a green labyrinth of secluded and foliated alcoves.

Damon strode through an avenue of illuminated dwarf trees toward a wide, canopied entry port. The outer hall was long and high, perhaps two or three stories of vaulted reach. A system of ramps traversed its height and length. One led gently upward from the entrance and was moving. He stepped on.

The ramp gave out to a room of still larger scale with staggered platforms and stages set asymmetrically across its expanse. Stands, keyboard consoles, vision screens dotted the floor, as did tables and chairs, branching singly and in groups off a central aisle.

At the far end in a curvilinear chair sat a man. Another empty chair adjoined. The man looked up as Damon walked toward him, a seemingly endless passage made in silence through a carpet that seemed knee-deep. Damon tried to focus on the man's eyes, but a primordial compulsion drew his gaze to the other's feet. At them was a large, wolfish animal, lounging in relaxed manner but with head up, ears erect, and eyes interestedly forward. Damon slowed his pace to take this in, now finding the long passage ending too soon.

The man held a book. That, at least, was reassuring—probably calculatedly so. Damon spared a moment for admiration of the adroit stage management. He was quite close to the man now, a man showing no outward divergence from humankind in general: tanned, golden haired, and wearing little. Perhaps nothing. Bare-chested and bare-legged he certainly was, and the table hid the rest. A library type not seen on Earth since Periclean days.

Damon stopped a few feet away, the table between them. Another good touch. The wolf kept its gaze on Damon and regarded him equably as the man looked up.

"I saw your campfire and hoped you would come."

He gestured to the chair beside him. "Would you join me?"

Damon sat down. His host tapped the book in his lap. "I've been reading my favorite poet. Perhaps we can get the library to make you a copy, if we can have the loan of your dictionary and a few literary works for the computer."

"You seem to have a working vocabulary already," Damon said.

The other looked up sharply, searching Damon's face for defensiveness. Damon was annoyed with himself. His choice of words had been meant to convey a rapid adaptation to the situation. Instead he had left room for a suspicion of sarcasm, and this outworlder was apparently sensitive to nuances of that sort.

On the credit side, Damon had just learned a good deal about his contact from the interchange.

The other seemed to realize this and relaxed into an amused smile, his hands pushing him back from the table. Damon noted that he was clothed after all, in shorts of a brief cut.

"We have a telepathic capacity," he agreed. "And you've been broadcasting among yourselves at a pretty brisk clip. Enough, as you say, to give us a working vocabulary. Not a literary one, though. Right now the library is picking up our conversation and juxtaposing your words against my linguistic referents. But for you to really use the library, we should feed it some of your reference and literary works. A dictionary certainly. And medical and scientific references. Then we can work in some poetic, perhaps even metaphysical, efforts if you have people of that bent and interest."

Damon had by now sat down and was shifting eagerly in his chair. "Your library should be a treasure house to us."

"There will be some limitations and blocks to your usage of it, of course. But we should like you to profit from it. And enjoy it."

There was a moment of silence, each looking at the other. The animal regarded Damon from its position at their feet. The man noticed and continued. "This is Kira. My name is Harrod Dan."

"Damon Hart. But then you know that."

"Only as you voiced it. I'm not probing, only skimming your surface thoughts to facilitate translation."

Damon's thoughts continued on those lines, and he voiced them. "You can see that I'm Alien Contact Officer for the *Fairbairn*. And yourself?"

The other laughed openly. "A person of this planet. I do pretty much speak for my fellows, if I follow your drift."

"We haven't seen any others. Are there many?"

"Humans? Roughly thirty thousand."

"On the whole planet? Or is this an outpost, a colony of some type?"

Harrod seemed amused at the question. "That's the whole planet. Seems like a good, balanced number, don't you think, considering the environment and the other species it makes room for? And, yes, this is our home and only world."

Damon shook his head and waved about him. "But this city—it was built to hold millions." The other nodded. "How did you get down to such a number?"

"We did it purposefully and for a good reason. This world as you now see it is its embodiment."

"But how? The agreements needed, the self-sacrifice . . ."

"Yes," Harrod Dan answered. "That, too."

Damon looked around him at the vaulted splendor, functional though it was, of the library, and the greater splendor that it held and that lay about it, and wondered that a race could give it up. A city so at home with its surroundings, so clean and wasteless. A wonder, still, to him and a reject to its builders.

Harrod sensed the thought.

"Why fall in love with a halfway measure? Cities can be built not to offend the ecology. Relatively. But what about their millions of inhabitants? And even the best of cities are a drain. They require too much to keep them going, on a sociological and psychological basis as well as from a resource outlook. Yet they have their functions, and this library is one, though it's largely a retrieval center now. There are terminals elsewhere, and they can produce a bio-degradable book on blank stock virtually on command.'' He tapped the volume on the table before him.

''Have you conquered the drive to reproduce, to perpetuate your culture?''

''Pretty much. It's a rather egregious form of vanity, you know.''

The animal stirred and shifted. She yawned and gave her long muzzle a shake before lowering it between her paws. Peace with the animal world, too. The millennium at last—but was it utopia or stasis? Or merely a stage to some higher level of development? Maybe the rationalization of an enervated race's decline? Damon shook his head groggily.

Harrod had followed Damon's shift of gaze toward the animal.

''There's more to the solution. I've already introduced you to Kira Sor. Let me do so again.''

Commander Bering kept his voice even but the tone hard. Apparently this was a confrontation he could afford, even wanted to force. His twang cut across the wardroom smoke, the words almost lazily drawn out, yet forceful.

''Let's pull back a moment from these fanciful disclosures and deal with a more workaday matter. If you would, Mr. Hart, explain to me the delay in reporting a contact of this importance. You met the native late last night, yet we hear of it now, some eight to ten hours later. Are we to be informed of these matters entirely at your leisure?''

Damon regarded the Exec and the other department heads with as much composure as he could muster. They regarded him from across the green baize of the wardroom table, now cleared of tablecloth, gaming paraphernalia, and other reminders of normal routine. Only the ashtrays remained. Some of the assemblage, all senior to Damon in rank and in years, surveyed him as a malleable jury follows the lead of an accusatory judge. Khan, Damon saw, was viewing the matter with somewhat less gravity. His left eyebrow lifted slightly as he caught Damon's glance sweeping by. The Captain seemed to be noncommittally allowing the Exec his scope.

Damon turned back toward the Exec. ''Not at my leisure, Commander. I reported to the Captain at the first opportunity to see him in person, and I'm reporting again now. I thought that might be more productive than a secondhand account relayed via radio, with all of you assembled in nightclothes.''

''Nightclothes be damned!'' A flush of choler suffused the Exec's face. He controlled it and passed on more evenly. ''The inconvenience of pulling on our pants aside, Mr. Hart—how can you justify not informing the Captain immediately? Or myself?''

''Commander,'' Damon stated crisply, and the others looked up, ''the ship was a continent away and beyond direct communication. The scout was five hundred miles away and due to pick me up in the early morning. I tried to raise it and failed. In any case, I would have said little.''

"And why is that, Mr. Hart?" the Captain interposed softly.

"Several reasons. I didn't want to relay a message via another hand that was so open to garbling and so apt to produce wild speculation. And then, I had been approached as a diplomatic equal, preferably of some responsible standing. That was an image worth preserving. I didn't want to trade that image for an errand boy's. Finally, this native has a self-admitted telepathic capacity, and we don't know its range. They admit openly to monitoring our communications. I didn't want to risk this sort of interchange under such circumstances.''

There was a momentary silence followed by a general fidgeting. Damon went on. "I think it most unlikely that he has the ability or inclination to keep my thoughts under long distance surveillance. I mean *now*. But if he does, better that we are in a more deliberative, reasoned state of mind. For the most part.''

Damon could hear the low hum of the air exchanger in the conversational void. The Captain broke it. "I agree, Mr. Hart, though your last remark was a bit gratuitous. But let's get on with it. The question is how we ought to receive this native. Or natives.''

"How many are there, really?" the Gunnery Officer ventured. "Can we credit their account? This Harrod Dan—and his wolfish companion—seem to be the sole representatives of the only intelligent species we've found here."

"Or who have found us," Damon responded. "Let me point out that Kira is human in all but bodily shape. She had that too, once."

"How do we know that the 'wolf' voice you received mentally wasn't this other native's?" the Exec pursued. "The human one, I mean. Some sort of telepathic ventriloquism." He traveled his smile over his sycophants, who chuckled dutifully. "Are all the fish and birds to be regarded as our mental equals? Or more? Could it be that you've been suckered, Mr. Hart?"

"Always possible, Commander. I had thought of that. But until we find this theory to be a fraud—if we ever do—we have to go forth on some basis. For ourselves as well as the natives, we have to define our objectives regarding this planet."

"Colonization," snapped the Exec. "Mineral exploitation. Even if we buy this fanciful theory, the bulk of the human inhabitants have departed—at least in human form. There's room for plenty more."

"A moment, Commander," Khan said from across the table. "From what we've heard, the planet lies so thinly populated through its inhabitants' choice. They could hardly look with favor on our trying to reverse that status.''

''There's another possibility,'' the Gunnery Officer said, emboldened by the Exec's support. ''This 'Harrod' could be among the remnants—possibly the last—of a declining race, forced back to a life of simplicity by lack of numbers or vitality rather than through choice. It could be a giant bluff.''

The Captain had seemingly had enough of this speculation. Swinging toward Damon, he took command of the discussion.

''We need more data. Mr. Hart, kindly extend to Harrod Dan—we ought to at least refer to him by the name he chooses—an invitation to visit the ship as my guest. His companion, too. Needless to say, there'll be no talk of colonization on such an occasion. In fact, we ought to consider other aspects of this planet. Aspects of high value. Aspects that this discussion hasn't touched on. I gather you're with me, Mr. Hart?''

''The library. It could contain a hundred technologies, a cancer cure, a dozen Shakespeares. Maybe a workable socioeconomic system. The histories and knowledge of a wealth of races and cultures.''

''All that and more,'' the Captain said. ''But we'll never know if we botch it. This will *not* be another Cygnus.'' He stood up and leaned forward, both hands grasping the table edge, no longer the moderator but the leader. ''So I direct that we receive

Harrod Dan with respect and open-mindedness, our only objective being to expand our knowledge. All political matters and policies are to be avoided.''

Not all present cared to meet his eyes. Some for the worthiest of reasons. Khan was casting inward—in philosophical, even spiritual thought, Damon guessed. Others, less nobly motivated, dreamt their petty fantasies of opportunism and personal advancement. The Captain took it in, then broke the reverie with curtness bordering on contempt.

''This meeting is dismissed!''

Harrod Dan chose to leave Kira behind. He appeared in a flowing robe that conveyed a distinct dignity, redolent of Roman senates and Athenian agoras.

The Captain met his guest at the companionway. After a brief introduction of his officers, he retired with Harrod to his quarters for refreshments. They emerged after an hour for a tour of the ship, Harrod as equable in expression as before. The Captain wore a look of bemusement and perhaps frustration.

Harrod maintained throughout his visit a cordial but aloof demeanor. He seemed hardly a guest at all. Upon being welcomed to the wardroom with a ceremonial toast, he responded with a polite but pointed welcome to his world.

Even the unperceptive drew a point from the courteous disinterest that he showed throughout the tour.

He showed mild but clear amusement at the unavoidably awkward detours around the navigational and combat control centers.

It was a performance effective in its understatement, capped by the arrival of Kira as the ceremonial farewells were made. She emerged from the woods to fall in at Harrod's heel as he descended the companionway ramp. Together they strode to the forest edge and vanished within.

A lot can happen in a week to make some people happy and others not. The doctor was both. He was one of the few on board capable of testing Harrod's mind transfer thesis—if the process was a technical one. Immediately after sick call he was off each day to the city, the ship having been moved to closer proximity. The doctor divided his time between the library and the main municipal hospital. The hospital was tantalizing. Administrative records showed it to be still in sporadic use, despite the city's desertion. In particular, neurosurgical procedures were still being carried out from time to time, seemingly by visiting surgeons. The doctor couldn't tell precisely what was being done because the nomenclature was often unfamiliar and the library had an access block on the subject. On the other hand, he was learning all sorts of things about humanoid pathology and treatment, enough to arouse his professionalism to the point of having little interest or time for shipboard politics.

Harrod was willing to talk about the sociological and philosophical aspects of the planet's transition—which currently took in several million mentalities poured into other receptacles: the Kindred. The few humans visible were the youngest on the planet. There were some spare human bodies available—a few people moving on early—but not many chose to do the same experience twice. There was no immortality here. To the contrary, there was an erosion factor plus some other limitations that Harrod would not elaborate on. Two or three transfers were all you got.

The interests of the Exec and the Gunnery Officer seemed elsewhere, and not capable of satisfaction at the library. After one or two frustrating expeditions, they gave up.

The geological survey teams were more or less up or down, as on any planet, depending on the day's find.

Khan counted himself a lucky man. Immersing himself in philosophy, poetry, and theology, he spent most of his free time at the library.

The crew in general was happy. There was a fresh, invigorating air to the planet, a vibrant, alive feel. All but the dullest fished, tramped the woods, and paddled the lakes on their liberty hours.

Damon was learning, but never quite enough. Knowledge was never tendered outright or available without effort. Harrod had made it politely clear that his people had only passing interest in the *Fairbairn* and its crew, extending to some assistance in its education through the library, and then only in directions that they deemed advisable. Not necessarily the directions the Terrans chose. Like the Exec and the Gunnery Officer, Harrod observed dryly.

When the Captain's gig exploded, it went in its entirety. No recording instruments, no debris, nothing remained to give a clue to the proximate cause. The atomics had seen to that.

There was plenty of reason, Damon thought, to believe that any investigation would have been less than thorough, no matter what. But there was nothing concrete on which to hang that sour supposition.

The Exec moved swiftly but circumspectly—as if he had been prepared? But, then, so should be all second officers. He took on command authority with an assured ease, yet showed an unexpected grace and tact toward those who regarded his accession with as much shock as they regarded the Captain's death. Damon wondered how long it would last. So did many another, but no one seemed eager to test the new Captain on points of sensitivity, first of which was the cursory investigation of the explosion.

"Why should they?" Khan asked when others tried to draw him into speculation. "Further inquiries would be fruitless, if not dangerous."

Some of these same officers considered the new

Captain's delicacy and consideration as a sign of complicity in the explosion. Khan had even less patience with them.

"Commander Bering's got his blind spots," he said to Damon. "But that doesn't necessarily make him the villain they'd like him to be. He'd act the same if the Captain had gone in his sleep. It's not only murderers who value a smooth transition."

"Sit down, Mr. Hart," said Commander Bering. There was only one place to sit, the straight-backed, uninviting chair across from the Captain. Damon looked around. It was his first visit to the Captain's sea cabin. It was more common by far for the Captain to move to his more sumptuous in-port cabin once planetfall had been made, where he could relax at ease and entertain local dignitaries, if any. Yet the new Captain had moved back to the sea cabin, chock-ablock to the bridge and its command control network. Not a good sign. Caution, even incipient paranoia, or the desire to set a Spartan example seemed the only possible motives.

The cabin was certainly spare enough: a bunk built into the bulkhead, and by the pillow a voice-actuated annunciator connecting with the bridge. A combination desk/chart table that swiveled to provide access from either the bed or a chair, padded a cut better than Damon's. The Captain occupied that chair now. Damon's chair, getting ever less comfortable beneath him, completed the cabin's furnishings.

"We will be leaving this planet shortly, Mr. Hart," the Captain said, leaning back in his chair as much as the modest upholstery would allow. "Sooner than is generally supposed. You will keep this intelligence to yourself."

Damon regarded the Captain and tried to lean back in his chair. He failed. He nodded instead.

"I will have an overall evaluation to make," the Captain went on. "As you know, it is an overview, meant to deal with the various aspects that characterize a planet. Some of them will be of interest to scholars here and there. But one aspect will be of interest to everyone on Earth. I mean, of course, the planet's suitability for colonization."

Damon gave up trying to sit comfortably. The tenor of the conversation made it doubly impossible. He concentrated on harnessing his emotions instead.

"I will draw, for this evaluation, from the reports of all concerned department heads, and their findings will supplement my report as addenda," the Captain continued didactically. In a position of unassailable power, he seemed intent on steamrollering over all objections. Damon didn't offer any. The Captain eyed him speculatively and pressed on. "Though this is your first report as a department head, I assume that you are familiar with the process."

Damon nodded again.

"Judging from a compatibility matchup, a resource evaluation, and so on, there can be little question of the suitability—the desirability—of the planet. Doubly so, when one throws in the cultural advantages that the library has to offer. The only question concerns the planet's inhabitants.'' The Captain paused again and regarded Damon with a quizzical half smile. ''How do you think they would take to such a prospect, Mr. Hart?''

''They wouldn't, Captain. They've sensed the intent and made it clear that we're welcome only as visitors.''

''Do you mean, Mr. Hart, that they feel proprietal or territorial about a world they've deserted? In human form, at least? Can you answer that from your relations with the handful that still remain?''

Damon felt a queasy twinge. He saw himself in an equally hard witness chair before a subcommittee of powerful men, all aware of his junior status and inexperience, being questioned by an intent advocate with an ax to grind.

''Territorial isn't the word, Captain. They regard this world more as a trusteeship.''

It was the Captain's turn to nod. A nod of dismissal.

''Do you believe this business of mind transmission, of miniaturization?''

Damon again tried unsuccessfully to lean back while selecting his words. No upholstery to give and the chair legs anchored to the deck. He managed the nearest approximation by crossing his legs and tilting his head.

''Yes, I believe it. I have no reason not to.''

''The doctor tells me that the library provides no data on the subject,'' the Captain offered equably.

''Harrod Dan says that the subject is proscribed.

Perhaps the process isn't surgical or medical at all. I haven't asked. Besides, I've communicated with Kira Sor.''

"Or someone you thought was the wolf," the Captain continued in his cross-examination mode. "It could have been the alien."

Inwardly Damon shook his head at the Captain's dehumanizing terms. *Wolf. Alien.* No names anymore.

"I should also like you to determine, Mr. Hart, whether these natives, however few or many there may be, have mental abilities over and above telepathic ones. Kinetic powers, for instance."

"You desire me to cover this in my report, Captain?"

"That, too. But I want to be personally briefed." The Captain paused and stressed his words. "Briefed as soon as you can personally determine the matter. Not at your discretion, as on past occasions. Is that clear?"

Damon gave another nod, the major component of his conversation with the Captain. The Captain continued. "Concerning your report: I desire a complete cultural and sociological evaluation of these people, as indeed regulations require. However, I do *not* desire you to embark on questions of policy, particularly of colonization. Your report is to be a scientific study. I will deal with political matters in my overview." The Captain said challengingly, "I would like there to be no misunderstanding on this point."

Damon looked down at his fingers, then up at the Captain.

"I understand you perfectly, Captain."

The Captain regarded him stonily. "Report to me, Mr. Hart, when you have the answers to the questions I raised. Kindly do it soon."

Damon got up—a painful process physically, if not mentally.

"I'll do that, sir. But perhaps you'd be better convinced if you raised the question with Harrod Dan yourself."

"I don't need convincing, Mr. Hart. And I have every confidence in your abilities. I will not see the alien before we leave."

"His mind's made up, Rachman. The idea of colonization is preposterous, from a power standpoint if not a moral one. But he doesn't seem to care. How can that be?"

Khan pulled on his pipe. "Because, Damon, the failure, if such it becomes, will be another man's. The Captain will get the plaudits for the discovery. And, within his narrow bailiwick, the rewards. Let someone else botch the job. Considering the relativity factor, it may be decades before the botching comes to light. Commander Bering could be an admiral on the retired list. Who knows?—perhaps both honored and buried by then."

Damon nodded morosely. Once more the cries and moans of a dice toss wafted across the wardroom. The winners and their backers slapped the table and guffawed.

"I bought a little time with my responses," Damon said. "I didn't contradict or challenge him directly, though he surely knows that his demands cut straight across the specific responsibilities of my position. I can't beg the colonization question in my report."

"Then why did you avoid the challenge?"

"Because otherwise I'd likely be relieved of my duties on some pretext or other."

"And what do you think will happen when you do, inevitably, have to submit your report?" Khan pursued.

"I think that the report and I will likely never reach home. There's a long time and a number of worlds still to visit, and I'm sure the Captain will see to it that some of them are dangerous. To me, at least." Damon paused. "As an alternative, I can write the report the Captain wants and repudiate it later."

"Given the correctness of your analysis, do you think that will save you?"

Damon took time to enjoy the luxury of being able to lean back in a chair again.

"Not really. I might be even a more likely candidate for an accident between the writing of such a report and a possible repudiation. Unless I had the repudiation written simultaneously and entrusted elsewhere."

"And you once called my suppositions Byzantine." Khan smiled. "But perhaps you overrate your importance. Given your lack of seniority and experience, your report would be vulnerable. As a handy strawman, it might survive. But either way, by your analysis, you would likely not.''

Khan in turn leaned back, puffing on his small ivory pipe. Damon found his fist clenching and for the first time in his life wished he were a smoker. He laughed instead, hoping it wouldn't sound like a nervous release.

This was a conversation of cross currents, revelations, and flux. Conflicts were stating their dimensions, but also resolving themselves. Loyalties sorted themselves out, though in novel and surprising realignments. And some novel and exciting possibilities hove into view. Some were downright frightening, though no less so than the current stasis.

"You know, Rachman, the Captain's driving me into an outright adversary position. A survival situation, to be precise. Harrod's more the ally.''

Khan held his response as an engineering officer passed nearby on a random search for boredom relief. Finding a magazine, he moved on.

Khan veered off on one of his verbal tangents.

"One thing, Damon. Don't consider that the Captain will be deterred by these people's telepathic abilities. You know that we've run into psi powers before. Anthony's World, for instance.''

"Part of our contact procedure stems from that

experience. But we backed off there. Anthony's World is off limits.''

''It is,'' Khan agreed. ''Largely because it's arid, windswept—in short, not desirable for colonization, its inhabitants' wishes or not. And there was never a chance to do a serious assay there. But that visit has steered a lot of money and scientific brainpower toward developing a thought screen or scrambler. That kind of obstruction or shield may be within our powers, even though we understand positive psi only lightly. We may find it developed when we get back.''

''I didn't know that,'' Damon said slowly.

''I think the Captain does. And until he learns of more fearsome powers than telepathic communication, he's not likely to run scared.''

River-cut and forested, the valley held a dwelling built among and around a family group of large conifers. Call it a tree house. It was hard to tell where tree left off and artifact began.

The distinction had seemed nonexistent from the air.

The skimmer's airstream buffeted the tree house's evergreen canopy as they approached an elevated landing stage, unseen till they hovered about it. Damon stood by the skimmer, watching the shafts of sunlight arrow past him and down through the curtain of greenery. Quiet—the natural state of such a place—ruled again. Their arrival sparked no great scurry of

activity. Harrod and Kira escorted them about, along
arcaded passages that spiraled around the massive
trunk to stages cantilevered out, almost random in
their placement and elevation. The adults that they
could see moved with an unhurried purposefulness.
The children showed less reserve. Damon felt light
tendrils of thought on his consciousness. Mischievous interrogatories directed elsewhere, not at him
and Khan. He smiled through it, trying not to look
inane.

All this was by the way. Side impressions. The
locus of their visit was the Council Room.

It was a small room and a small gathering. Harrod
sat down in an upholstered chair and motioned
Rachman and Damon to do the same. Kira made for
a raised platform, almost a dais, across the room.
Large perches lined the walls. One was occupied by
a large accipiter who ruffled his wing feathers at their
arrival and eyed them piercingly. Two other natives
occupied chairs scattered in seeming haphazard fashion.

But, somehow, the room was filled.

A welter of interacting minds, cross-connecting in
intricate patterns, woven through the air as the breeze
swept and eddied through inlets of its own. Damon
felt tendrils, intimations of heavy, oily, rolling bodies in ocean-deep waters: thoughts deep but never
ponderous. Other minds that sang as they thought.
Soaring, circling minds, unwillingly brought to earth-
bound concerns. And most strangely and inexplica-

bly, minds with no corporeal referent but sharp and with an impress of their own.

The thoughts had many variations, but one commonality: *You cannot stay.*

Harrod read the impression on Damon's mind. "The Council speaks of the ship's presence. You are welcome to stay. From our view it is desirable. I had planned to suggest it, but did not want to force a test of your loyalties until you had defined them for yourself."

Damon nodded but held silence. Khan spoke out from the depths of his chair:

"I think that Damon is still sorting out his loyalties. Perhaps we can make it easier."

Damon felt the touch of Kira's thoughts: cool, feral, feminine. *You need not regard staying with us as a betrayal of your beliefs or your people, Damon. And I say that not as a mere point of persuasion. We have decided to permit access to our world, its libraries, its forests, to those of your world who would learn from it, not seek to exploit it. And when that first study party—and we do mean nonmilitary party— arrives and then leaves, we will encourage you to go back with it as an interpreter, an ambassador of our way. And you will go back with abilities you never believed you possessed.*

Damon looked across the room at Kira, then at Harrod. Harrod smiled, as if enjoying a jest while proffering a gift.

"Kira means that you and most humans possess the capacity for telepathic communication and more. You have not tried in the right way. You must be supported, so to speak, by the group and paraded through the motions until you can do it yourselves. But the ability is there—as is the ability to write with the left hand, were you shown how and applied yourselves."

"A princely offer," Khan said. "One that I would gladly accept in your place."

"But not in yours."

"Rachman's responsibilities are of a different order," Harrod said. "He and I know that, and you have come to suspect it. He can counterbalance your Captain's advocacy within higher circles and with far more power than you can within yours."

"Even were I to accept, I wouldn't want to do it as a deserter, simply sneaking away. It's not a role or label I'll willingly accept."

Harrod turned to Khan on an abruptly different conversational slant. Or so it seemed to Damon.

"Your name holds interesting nuances and overlays. 'Rachman' and 'Khan' are straightforward enough. The third part, though—'Pindharee'?"

"It had meaning once," Khan said. "Relating to long ago ancestry. Outlaw, warlord, outsider, bandit. Interesting shades of distinction. Particularly to any who happened to confront someone in such a personification." Khan paused and looked at Damon. "Of course, time has stripped the emotions from such associations now. The name is simply a label, a vestige of a colorful past.''

"A nice point," Damon said. "Still, I won't have the cushion of centuries between myself and what I'm called. I can live with that, though. What I'd like is to make my leaving more than a limited personal act. I'd hope to give it some larger weight.''

Harrod cocked his head, and Damon sensed the input of other minds before he spoke again.

"A good thought—and we can actually use the occasion to make a point. There are several points we want to make to your Captain and, through him, to your world. And I'm afraid that with a man of his makeup, the points will have to be backed with a show of force.''

"He won't agree to meet you.''

"Then we will make him do so. I think that just the kind of demonstration to make our point—to be the point itself. Or one of them. We will offer him a choice of compliance or loss of face. That he can understand.''

"You can really carry that out?''

Again Damon felt a wave of *other* presence, other minds that had withdrawn from the colloquy but that now surged back. Thoughts weighted with determination and power, but counterpointed also with mischievous laughter.

"Oh, yes," Harrod said. "We can carry it out. One day you shall, too."

Damon cleared the skimmer from the treetop canopy, banking in a slow wheel before heading into the sun and the city over the horizon.

"An interesting glimpse at your culture. Or one shard of it. I wish we could have done that sooner."

Kira and Harrod offered no response. Behind Damon, Khan sat abstractedly, smoking a dark cheroot.

The greenery flowed below them like a moving carpet. Damon took his time in choosing his words.

"I was very impressed by the Council meeting." He paused. "But then, I think we were meant to be."

Harrod kept a sober face, but Kira let her amusement flow openly.

"A bit of what we would call a dumb show," Khan added judiciously from the rear seat. "Your world's equivalent. Gestures for speech. Speech for thought. Thought for . . . maybe something beyond. I don't doubt the seriousness of those deliberations, but I'll agree with Damon that there was somewhat more than had to be. And in some ways somewhat less than the whole reality. Perhaps the smoke and gestures were to draw off our perception of what was happening. Or lacking."

Damon throttled back a bit. The lake was coming

up at them, a glistening pool of quicksilver. The city towered above it on the far shore, distant still.

"I've learned one thing about your culture. Learning is a working process. You don't deliver insights or data gratuitously."

"Quite right," Harrod agreed amiably. "But that's also true among ourselves—our young and even the not young. Not only when dealing with outworlders, and you're far from the first of those. Of course, we sometimes do go further. We make no show of overt weapons, so we may have to resort to a bit of misdirection."

But not completely, Kira put in. *Not among friends. That was a genuine Council meeting, though not in the form we would usually hold it these days. That was a mode of assembly once, in more complicated but less advanced times. Nowadays we would do it a bit differently.*

"Some of the Council appreciated it, though," Harrod said. "It was an interesting return to a kindly remembered tradition."

And the deliberations were serious ones, the decisions seriously rendered. Do not doubt that.

"There was something more," Khan added. "Something that the show and 'smoke' were meant to obscure. I think it had to do with the *essence* of some of the participants."

"Right again," Harrod said. "It's hard to tell whether you two are becoming more psi sensitive in such a short time or are simply quite observant. The two are not completely apart, not in our culture. And weighing your sensitivities was indeed a less open purpose of this meeting.''

Despite Damon's light hand on the acceleration and his long banking turns, the city was looming large ahead. He swung the craft to the lee of a crystal-faceted tower, swooping out and low over the lake.

''I imagine that once again you will leave us to fit the pieces to the puzzle in our own time.''

''You'll have time. Rachman on the trip back. You in the years to come.''

Damon found the night to be free of second guessing but full of apprehensions. Perhaps *anticipations* was a better word.

He was amazed at how few affairs he had to clear up. He had a report to write. He wrote it, burnished it, and transcribed it against a background of Beethoven and Rodrigo.

After, he lay in his bunk letting the music wash him, touch him with waves of orchestration, tendrils of guitar arpeggios, engulfing crescendoes. He fell asleep—a dreamless sleep—and the night was over.

There were some who enjoyed standing the quarterdeck as in-port OOD, and Lt. Arthur Snyder was one of them. His uniform was starched, and he carried the ceremonial long glass under his arm, a faintly ridiculous latter-day Hornblower.

Usually boring, the watch did have its serious sides. In many ports there lay the real threat of attack, sometimes open and sometimes under peaceful guise. The in-port OOD had sophisticated weaponry, nuclears included, at his command.

The quarterdeck could also be a petty fiefdom with a four-hour reign. Snyder seemed to regard it so. As Harrod waited composedly, Snyder met Damon's arrival on deck with a lofty mien.

"Come off it, Art," Damon said exasperatedly. "What do you mean I can't take him below?"

"Look for yourself," Snyder said. "Your own fault if you don't keep up with the Captain's standing orders."

Damon eyed Snyder sharply. Though a jg and nominally junior in rank, Damon no longer stood in port watches, while full lieutenants like Snyder did. The resentment showed.

Damon walked over to the logbook. There it stood:

"While on this planet, entry to this ship shall be denied to all but ship's company. The OOD shall, with all due courtesy, refuse entry to all others on the basis of orders from higher authority. No elaboration on the term 'higher authority' shall be proffered. Such higher authority shall be officially unavailable to countermand said orders. All visitors shall be turned away with this explanation, and a report of the incident forwarded directly to the Captain immediate upon the visitor's departure.

"If the visitor shall refuse to depart, after all diplomatic handling of the situation is pursued, the OOD shall employ such force as is necessary to deny entry to the ship."

Damon glanced over to Harrod, who nodded his appreciation of the situation. Damon turned back to the OOD.

"I'm going below to see the Captain, Art."

Even so tunnel-visioned an officer as Snyder was becoming aware of the tensions building. And on his watch! His demeanor and uniform began to wilt. Damon turned away. He made it a short passage to the Captain's quarters, with one brief stop on the way at the marine office.

The Captain received Damon promptly, waving him to the same iron maiden of a seat as before. Damon winced and sat down. He waited until the Captain's orderly had closed the hatch behind him.

"Harrod Dan would like to see you, Captain. He's at the quarterdeck now."

"So Lieutenant Synder has told me. And I've told *you* that I shall not see him again. If he has anything to say to me, he can put it in writing or relay it via your offices."

Damon eyed the Captain appraisingly. He seemed to be up for this encounter. Though under tight control, his nostrils showed a slight flare, his face a flush of fresh blood. The Captain drew his lips into an impatient frown.

"I've made it more than plain, Mr. Hart. I have told you that we're leaving shortly. I'll tell you now that we lift off tomorrow. I do not choose to believe this native to be representative of anyone but himself. He's shown me nothing to the contrary. It is true he apparently has telepathic capabilities. For that reason I do not choose to make him privy to decisions that are best carried out without advance declaration. So I shall not see him, and you may regard that as final."

"A Captain is master on his ship," Damon said carefully. "I don't lightly contradict him. Yet this ship is on Harrod Dan's world, and his message is that he is master of this world—Harrod and those of his people."

"That remains to be seen, Mr. Hart."

The statement challenged Damon as well as Harrod, and he responded sharply. "Harrod will see you, sir, on his terms if necessary. He is offering you the choice of a voluntary meeting or a forced one."

Damon awaited the explosion. The Captain surprised him. Leaning back in his chair—a feat Damon envied—he lazed an arm over its back and smiled.

"Does he plan to force his way in?"

"No, sir. He intends to force you to come to him."

The Captain considered. "Let him try. If he can

get me to the hatch, I'll go the rest of the way under my own steam.''

The Captain eyed Damon confidently, challengingly.

There was a lurch and a scrape of metal, and the Captain was on his feet, his face a study in struggle, fear, and hostility. His legs moved jerkily, and he slapped at them with both hands in a spastic attempt at beating them back. Then, with a lapse into a more natural gait—whether enforced or of capitulation, Damon didn't know—he took the few steps left to the hatchway.

"That will do," he said tautly. "I will come to the quarterdeck."

The quarterdeck was getting densely populated. At center stage was Snyder, pacing restlessly but now without pomp or long glass. All starch had departed his uniform and countenance. He stopped in his pacing for a fleeting glance at the clock. Twenty minutes stood between him and the salvation of the relieving watch. He had been clearly hoping that Damon would disappear to his stateroom to think things over, or to the Captain's cabin to talk things over—preferably at length. Any place, so long as the process used up the watch. Catching sight of Damon and the Captain he wilted still further, at the same time halting his pacing and attempting to come to attention. It made for a grotesque spectacle.

In the wings, as if awaiting their cues with varying degrees of interest or lack of it, were several others:

Haynes, the young watch messenger; he looked toward anything, even of a dangerous nature, that would relieve the boredom of the watch. Schultz, a stolid quartermaster who had seen it all. Khan, standing quite still in neatly pressed khakis that seemed to have absorbed Snyder's starch by transmigration. Khan's orderly, a rough-looking marine corporal, nonetheless expert in unobtrusiveness when the occasion demanded it. Harrod Dan, the nexus of the crisis, equally still, even diffident.

The Captain had worked much of the emotion from his face on the passage to the quarterdeck. A bare residue of self-irritation remained. He had wanted to avoid this confrontation altogether, but would rather have had it, if forced on him, in the privacy of his cabin. But his own standing orders had foreclosed that possibility without losing face on deck. His bluff called, he appeared at the gangway under tight control but clearly in an ugly mood. His furrowed forehead and downturned mouth showed his distaste at finding a larger assemblage than desired on deck. He took the initiative nonetheless.

"As you were, Mr. Snyder," he said with a dismissive glance, sending the OOD relievedly to the sidelines. He turned toward Harrod. "Good morning to you. I understand that you wanted to see me."

"Yes indeed, Captain. I understand that you're leaving tomorrow. I wanted to wish you farewell."

There was a rustle of interest on the part of the

watch messenger, the quartermaster, and, despite his
rigidity, the marine corporal, who had no prior notion of this news. Khan seemed unconcerned.

"Yes," the Captain said stiffly. "I appreciate your
courtesy and hospitality during our call here. I shall
further express my appreciation in my report."

"I hope you'll express rather more, Captain,"
Harrod said. "I have been instructed by our Council
to state explicitly that we shall receive such scientific and academic missions as Earth cares to send.
They are to be of a nonmilitary nature. Anything
larger in scope or permanence, anything that smacks
of a colony, is out of the question." He paused and
added, "If any explanation is required, over and
above the principle of sovereignty and the power to
back it up—which I'm afraid your culture prefers
over philosophical appeals to equity—let me say that
we did not contain our own population and restore a
fragile ecology in order to see that balance shattered
by others."

The Captain seemed discomfited. Though saying
what he did not mean was not his strong suit, the
situation demanded that he try.

"You must know that I do not make policy. I
carry it out. My job is to collect data, observe, and to
bring the ship home safely with those findings. At
most, I recommend."

"That won't do, Captain," Harrod said softly.
"You intend to lobby for your recommendations.

That's your privilege. But you are also an ambassador, and as such we intend that you relay our wishes along with your contentions. And we intend that your observations be more than self-serving.''

"I shall draw my own conclusions," the Captain said tartly.

"As long as others may do so as well."

At the mention of "others," the Captain shifted his gaze, skipping quickly over the men of assorted rank and station grouped on the quarterdeck, alighting lastly on Damon.

"You're who he means, I suppose," he said sharply. "I hold you responsible for this misunderstanding, Mr. Hart. You are relieved of duties and are confined to quarters. Lay below!"

"I think not, Captain," Harrod interposed.

With a great effort at self-control, the Captain turned toward him.

"This is not your affair. Kindly remember that this is my ship."

"And my world."

"Let's cut this short, Captain," Damon said. "I'm not laying below. I'm resigning from the service. I'm leaving this ship. You call it what you like. Frankly, I'm concerned for my welfare, even my life. There are other reasons as well, but I don't expect you to hold still for a recital of them. You'll find them in my letter of resignation. Let's just say that I'm leaving."

The Captain turned briskly to the OOD. "Call the Master at Arms, Mr. Synder. Have him lay up to the quarterdeck with two men."

Snyder stood paralyzed. A frightened expression spread over his features, and his forehead beaded with sweat. Still he didn't move.

"Damn it, man! Obey your orders!"

"He can't," Harrod said.

The Captain whirled toward Khan. "Have your orderly take Mr. Hart into custody."

Khan turned to the corporal. "Place Mr. Hart under arrest."

The corporal's oafish astonishment turned also to fear as he ordered his body to respond. The only sign of function was a spreading stain of sweat at the armpits.

Harrod stepped forward, his diffident manner gone completely. Still the Captain held his ground. Harrod confronted him face to face but spoke clearly and loudly, as if to ensure that all within reach could hear and understand.

"Captain Bering, I've given you our message. As a responsible officer whose duties include ambassadorial functions, you will relay that message. I tell you further that no crew member will be able to operate a weapon on this world. Any officer ordering such action, yourself most particularly included, will be restrained. Killed, if necessary. Any attempt to retaliate with weapons once clear of this planet will meet with the same result." He paused. "I have given you a demonstration of our abilities. And more, you have given me the chance to demonstrate those abilities before—through—the men around us. Kindly remember that."

"Kindly leave this ship!" the Captain rasped harshly.

Damon strode to the quartermaster's table and laid an envelope on it.

"My letter of resignation, Captain. To BuPers, for transmittal by you. As regulations require."

Harrod was already at the off ramp. With a last nod to Khan, Damon followed.

The Captain watched the retreating figures, his face stolid but his fingers working. The high sun shone on Harrod Dan's bare shoulders, unreflected by perspiration. But the Captain noted with the small shred of satisfaction left to him that Damon Hart's uniform shirt was as soaked as any of the others.

The Captain eyed the deck chronometer, then turned to the OOD. Snyder had not dared to move, even once he could.

"Mr. Snyder!" the Captain snapped, and waited till the lieutenant had stiffened to attention. "Enter in the ship's log that at 1130 local time, Lieutenant jg Damon Hart deserted the ship. Attempts at dissuading and restraining him were futile."

* * *

The ramps were secured, the hatches closed. There was no sign of activity. The ship seemed an inert behemoth, beached and dead on an unlikely strand.

There was life inside, most of it preoccupied with the routine of departure. Perhaps a few felt pangs or other wrenches at leaving.

Kira and Harrod stood by Damon, beyond him in thought, and linked to a departing kindred spirit in a manner Damon could only imagine and one day hope to attain. Cortald Dir: stowaway, potential ambassador, enforcer.

The ground beneath the ship began to creak as mass and weight shifted, then lifted off. The ship rose slowly, tilting upward. The propulsion motors cracked on with explosive force. With increasing velocity the ship accelerated to a small point, then disappeared.

A long, ovoid depression in the ground, crushed grass and sod, were the reminder of what had been.

Damon turned first toward the forest edge. Harrod Dan and Kira Sor followed.

Part II

TURNAROUND

Damon felt the weight of eleven years of expectancy lift as the ship lowered its bulk to the meadow's green. A probability was becoming a reality.

Damon *felt* the ship settle, felt it as the hull sensors flashed the data down the electronic circuits to the data banks and processors. The computer responded with minor feedback impulses, positioning the ship to stability before shutting down the lift motors.

Strange, seeing and *feeling* a landing as the ship's nerve center experienced it. There would come a day—not far off—when a man's brain would interlink with the computer, not merely direct it. In a sense it was happening now. Damon was doing it. There wasn't true sentience to touch. Damon was in admiration of an almost autonomic function, his link with the shipboard computer a lesser thing than the higher level linkage of true consciousness going on about him.

He was the tag end of the parade. Cortald Dir was coming home.

Home. Damon felt the long grass switch his legs lightly as he shifted position in the meadow. It was a finer grass than that of Earth. Not as sword-edged and dense as that of his boyhood memories.

What memories? He had seldom strode through meadow grass as a boy. If he had, it was to retrieve an overthrown baseball or to detour past a vicious dog. He would have paid no mind to the tactile sensations of the grass. These home memories were mostly idealizations, distillations of experiences, not all of them his.

Kira leaned her flank against his leg. Bristly fur prickled his skin.

Was home where you came from or the place where you longed to return? Or visit for the first time? What was home to an out-of-body being like Cortald Dir? A developmental stage or two yet to come, and Cortald would disappear as a personality perceptible to those still behind, even the noncorporeal ones. He would be gone. Part of the universal essence but still—so far as Damon could understand it—with an identity not totally annihilated. But gone nonetheless from mankind's ken.

Cortald Dir was back now. Voyager, preparer, safeguard—those roles were past now. A throng of others greeted him, melded with him. Damon, the Once Born, Kira and the other Kindred—all could just nibble on the crumbs. The greatest depth of the interplay was beyond Damon. He zeroed in on the computer's more mundane functions and Cortald's imprint on them.

Damon doubted that he would ever function as a ship's officer again. Yet, pursuing the cybernetic neural pathways, he knew that he could land, could navigate, could *be* the ship in a symbiotic meld that no ship's navigator had ever reached. He longed to try.

You will, Damon. Kira's thoughts impinged ever so lightly. Kira believed in old times' sake and the first perception of new times to come. She had let him work through both. *You'll fly that ship, be that ship. And they'll never know.*

It was an exciting prospect, but not without its deprivation. He would do all that, but as a part of leaving this world. Of going home. Or leaving home.

Not for a couple of years. Let it sort itself out. Don't push it.

Damon nodded and tried to focus on the realities nearer at hand. There were people on that ship, some of whom would stay here those couple of years. Folk of scientific bent. For the most part.

It was their other part that intrigued Damon the most.

Ships are as much passageways as places. Damon knew every step of the passages and lifts that led from the quarterdeck to the Captain's cabin. No matter—Damon was not ship's company, very definitely *not* ship's company. As a consequence, he was being escorted by the OOD's watch messenger.

Damon doubted that this ship's company knew much of him. This messenger looked peach-fuzz young, probably on his first tour of duty off-world. He had likely been in a crib teething on rubber toys when Damon had last seen Earth. Damon bore the stamp of *different*. Did such a boy understand the notion of going native? Desertion, yes. Alienness, yes. Damon was something unclassifiable, maybe in between. For whatever reason, his escort kept his distance, walking briskly ahead and not making eye contact at any stage of their traverse of the ship's innards. Damon walked more deliberately, in light sandals, forcing the messenger to slow occasionally so as not to widen the distance embarrassingly.

The Captain had chosen to receive Damon in his in-port cabin, more commodious and inviting than the cramped sea cabin that Captain Bering had preferred. That augured favorably.

The hatch closed behind Damon, and the Captain rose from his chair behind his desk. His face was roughly modeled—craggy might have been a more polite way of putting it—with steady but not hostile blue eyes. He wore no cap in his cabin, but his summer tans were freshly creased and laundered. His eyes swept Damon, seeing what? A thirty-six-year-old lieutenant jg in a chitonlike robe and ankle-thonged sandals? A deserter? Or a foreign dignitary?

Damon risked a quick probe and got back a reflective mental flash of his own physical appearance, no judgmental attachments. That argued for a mind under tight control or one already made up.

"Come in and sit down, Mr. Hart," the Captain invited. The chair before the desk was upholstered and far more inviting than that Captain Bering had favored.

The Captain extended his hand and Damon took it. It was firm and warm.

"Welcome aboard, Mr. Hart. May I offer you a glass of sherry?"

"I'd like that," Damon said, easing into the chair.

The Captain reached for the crystal decanter on his desk. Judging from the frosty look of its cut facets, it was likely set on light chill. The Captain poured judiciously into two small, stemmed glasses on a filigreed silver tray adjoining and passed one over.

"To the taste of Earth," the Captain said, inclining his glass toward Damon.

Damon nodded and rolled the liquid in the glass, appraising its color. He took his first sniff and then a

sip. A flood of memory and feeling resonated through
his mind. Nutty aroma, redolent of hot sun and dark
soil. A slight metallic tang and overlay.

"Manzanilla?"

The Captain nodded.

"A nice gesture."

The Captain regarded Damon over his glass, still
held before him.

"I'll ask a gesture in return."

Damon looked up.

"No more probes," the Captain continued.

"You caught the one when I came in."

"Yes. I can't probe you, but I can pick up when
I'm being probed. I'd rather we talked on a basis of
equal access to each other."

Damon nodded agreement. Interesting—apparently
psi research had produced results already on Terra as
Khan had foretold. Was the Captain an exception, an
anomaly, or were there many with awakened psi
sensitivities back home?

"I'll have to ask, then, as to how I stand with the
government and with you," Damon said. "I recognize you for what you are, Captain of this ship. But
you have the advantage unless you tell me how you
view me."

"Fair enough. Officially, your resignation has never
been accepted. Nor have you been tried *in absentia*,
though desertion charges have been filed. It's still a
democratic government, and my guess is that this

status is to give them a legal handle on you, should you want to return home and turn out to be a trouble-maker. So far as I'm concerned, my orders are to provide you with passage home if you desire it. You'd be a passenger, almost though not quite a civilian. You would not be under arrest, but you'd be bound by ship regulations to the extent of any pas-senger. A tech rep, for example. I would not issue you any direct orders unless I felt that your presence or actions constituted a danger to the ship or its crew. Be warned, though—I've been given a high degree of latitude and will interpret that mandate quite liber-ally in my favor should I feel even indirectly threatened.''

"But you're not going home directly."

"No. We're near the end of a standard exploration loop, tangential to that of the *Fairbairn*. We're to penetrate and explore farther, then return in what will be two standard years here to pick up the scientific party. Yourself, too—if you want to return.''

"I'll defer my decision till then." Damon raised his glass, judiciously appraising the tawny color again. "This makes a strong affirmative argument."

"I don't doubt it," the Captain grinned. "Now—shall I see if I can assemble the scientists? The sooner they get acclimated the better. And they might well start with meeting you."

"Not shipboard," Damon said. "There's a better place."

*　　*　　*

The group was as nonmilitary as they come. Still, as they approached the library, four on foot behind an older man in a power sled, they reminded Damon of a platoon of infantry advancing behind the cover of a tank. Absurd imagery; the power sled was really nothing more than a sophisticated prosthetic conveyance. The formation was more likely a matter of deference to age and reputation.

Damon recognized the weathered face. Rune Stenmark had done his seminal work in his youth, while Damon was in grade school—or earlier. His intent look, the iron-hard feel of his mind, contrasted sharply with a failing body that even modern technology could maintain but not restore. He ran a distinct risk, perhaps a probability, of dying on this world. So far could the quest for understanding drive the best of men. A theoretical physicist, in his field he was the best. The four others in his wake were unknown quantities.

As Damon was in part to them. He doubted if they had been told all elements of his story. Even had they, he was a different quantity than the young jg, who had walked away from their world three of their years ago, eleven of his. They would know something of what he had been. They could only guess— some of them perhaps fear—what he was now. They advanced on an alien city, uninhabited but not dead,

nd a once known but somehow transformed Terran.
No wonder they advanced slowly.

Damon knew the feeling. It was his turn to be the
eception committee, as Harrod Dan and Kira Sor
ad been to him. He seldom visited the library anymore. Distant terminals provided access when he
eeded it. Yet there was a restful feeling of sanctuary
o what a library conceptually was, particularly when
coming from a workaday arena of strife and competi-
ion. That remained a distant legacy of his, but a
earer one to these newcomers.

The scout that had transported the scientists lifted
off, leaving them alone with Damon and the city.
Damon went forward to meet them along the trellised
walkway from the landing stage where he had once
set down his skimmer with hope and trepidation.

The older man propelled his sled forward. The
more able-bodied trailed behind.

Stenmark stopped before Damon. A stray breeze
uffled his fine gray hair. His eyes looked on Damon
with expectation. Damon read the eagerness and curiosity of youth.

"Welcome to this world, Dr. Stenmark. We'll try
o make your years here good ones."

"I have few years left, Mr. Hart."

A statement. And a question.

"We'll make them quality years, Doctor."

And that begged the question. Quantity. Hope for
more. Apparently they'd chosen to tell their scientists

some of the promises of the *Fairbairn* expedition.
Damon had been afraid they wouldn't. Perhaps the
offer of potential access to an extended life had been
the trade for production and loyalty. Not outright.
That would be too naked and impossible of enforce-
ment. Reciprocity, a sense of obligation—that would
be the touchstone to a man of Stenmark's known
ethics and integrity.

It might be other things to the rest. Power—the
power of acquired knowledge. Not unique here, but
enough to put a man at the top of his field on his
return to Earth.

There'd be time enough later for this type of delv-
ing. Others more skilled would do it. Damon raised
his gaze to embrace the whole group.

"You know who I am, and I recognize Dr.
Stenmark. He was a known figure before I left Earth.
You're all younger and unfamiliar. How about some
names and data to match the faces?"

The newcomers advanced their names and selves
with diffidence. No—not that; reluctance. Not all of
them exhibited the direct eagerness to embrace the
unknown that Stenmark had shown. Perhaps the in-
quiring spirit—and he hoped that, at least, was there—
bowed to the basic caution that marked all survival-
oriented mankind.

He sensed also a group fear and distaste—that this
was a charade. That Damon could learn what he
wanted by other means and that their words would be

mpty mouthings. It was too soon to acknowledge
he correctness of this suspicion.

Five packets of data, then:

1) *Observed:* Caucasian male, early forties. Lean,
but lacking good muscle tone. Pomaded hair.
Arms too long for sleeves. Self-conscious of
movement. Probably never outgrew childhood
reputation for clumsiness. Nor some of the clumsiness. Perhaps didn't care. Perhaps did. Clumsiness was a particularly negative value in his
culture.
Spoken: ''Roger Chabron. Mathematician and
cyberneticist.''
Surface reading: Gallic suspicion, a self-fulfilling
preconception. Distrust of Damon. Distrust of
words. Preference for mathematical symbols.
Yet, not a mathematical theorist of the top
rank, and knowing it. Proud of his chips-and-
circuits practicality. Need to defend importance
of own work, but suspicious that his mathemat-
ics were along as a handmaiden to Stenmark's
physics, and his self as a sop to his power bloc.

2) *Observed:* slim, sinewy, alert Caucasian female,
middle thirties. Copper hair. Skin bronzed, not
yet weathered. She probably made the distinction and cared. Took care of herself as best she
could—but work, even in harsh environments,

came first. Usually. Attractive to Damon, and firm: physically, mentally.

Spoken: "Kerry Burns. I'm an ethnologist, an anthropologist. When I can find anthropoids. Xenologist, otherwise."

Surface reading: challenging awareness of him as a male. No fear of the unknown there. Relish in the overlay of alien culture on attractive (to her) stock. Damon had to make a real effort to keep his awareness from showing—from facial coloring to an outright erection. He switched his gaze rapidly.

3) *Observed:* tall, self-effacing Indo-Aryan male of indeterminate age. Hair black, still with high luster. Dark brown eyes and skin, accentuated by garments of a linen white.

Spoken: "Vijay Chaudhuri. Semanticist." Damon raised a questioning eyebrow. Surely those who had planned the expedition knew that there'd be little need for such. Though perhaps not. Recognition of nuance, word and thought linkage could have its value even in a largely nonverbal society. "Student of literature," Chaudhuri continued shyly. "And sometimes poet."

Surface reading: highly developed esthetic sense. Sense of cultural perspective, possibly rivaling Kerry Burns', whose field it was. And Damon's. Disdain for the political. Damon gave the expedition's planners higher marks than he had first awarded. He saw the hand of Rachman Khan Pindharee, or someone like him.

4) *Stenmark:* in an intellectual class by himself. Already self-introduced.

5) *Observed:* intent, observant, sharp-featured male in middle forties. Precise movements and appreciation of the movements of others. Direct and challenging gaze.

Spoken: ''Malcolm Gant, M.D. My field's neurophysiology, psychobiology. And make it 'Mac' instead of 'Malcolm.' ''

Surface reading: precision going beyond the scientific. Carryover to personal realm. A tightly organized and disciplined mind. High awareness of hierarchical relationships. Adaptive to same. Manipulative, too. Almost certainly military. *Awareness of Damon's probe.* A slight smile of reaction and acknowledgment of Damon's appreciation. Definite psi sensitivities, way above normal. Seemed to be of a shielding, defensive nature—at the least. A certain tact here. He said nothing that would clue the others to the nature of this interchange.

Gant could be the watchdog of this scientific party. It was an open question as to where his loyalties were strongest. Or whether they were susceptible to change as Damon's had been.

This was definitely *not* the time to develop these

notions in depth, nor to stand around in wordles communion.

Damon took a half turn toward the library entrance

"Let's check out the library and the data retrieva system. It's got a sophisticated Terran vocabular: now—you can request, interrogate, get readouts, with no problem once you know the methodology."

The reception hall was imposing. Damon had for gotten his first impressions of its grandeur. One race' vaulted halls could well be another's head-bumping crawlways. But among all humans, at least, thi spelled splendor.

Damon led the way, the others trailed behind Little small talk. To be expected when being lec through the greatest repository of knowledge in the known worlds by a guide of suspect reputation and unknown powers. There was a distinct overlay o apprehension, more than an extension of the group': early caution and reluctance. Damon could pinpoin it now. The focus was Gant. The medical doctor dic stand—or walk—a bit apart. Or perhaps he had beer cut out from the herd. That tended to confirm the security connection, and that Gant had been at no great pains to hide it. That would be consistent with his power drive. Damon filed it away for late. investigation.

The group listened to Damon's run-through of the data retrieval system. Chabron showed the most in terest, probing beyond method to function. Damon

ained it in when it got too specialized. The subject
may have been Chabron's prime study, he reminded
him, but it was Damon's present job merely to show
him how to go about it.

"Are there access blocks, Mr. Hart?" Stenmark
asked from his sled.

"Yes. They're more complicated than you've been
led to believe. None is absolute. Put baldly, the library reads you when you request information. It
might provide access to any one of you and not
another, though the query might be the same. It
might permit access at a future time to a person
denied earlier."

Malcolm Gant pursed his lips. "Subjective evaluation? By a machine?"

"Yes indeed. We're very readable, you'll find."

"By you, too?" Kerry Burns asked. Damon looked
toward her to gauge her seriousness and found a
smile of mischief.

"Yes, if I choose."

"Does the library impose any blocks on you, Mr.
Hart?" Stenmark asked.

"No. Not that I know of. Though perhaps I don't
ask for information it wants to interdict."

"Then perhaps we can stimulate you to ask for
us," Vijay Chaudhuri ventured with a smile of white
on brown. Damon flashed back to a freeze-frame of
Khan.

"You'll find that the library will supply information only up to your capacity to absorb. It will educate you along the way, taking you back to simple or perhaps undiscovered concepts till you can grasp the data you think you want. Don't ask for a unified field theory, Dr. Stenmark, or a cure for cancer, Dr. Gant. You have to earn your way to such lodestones—if they do indeed exist. And you won't know that till you learn to evaluate. And satisfy the computer that you can."

"Interesting," mused Chabron in low tones. He sucked on an unlit pipe that he had produced as they walked. He was willing to stay on and play at testing his limits then and there. He'd roll out a sleeping bag, if he'd had one, or sleep atop a table for the night.

"You've got two years, Dr. Chabron," Damon reminded him. "Why don't we stick with getting all of you settled in, and consider that a good day's work."

The pillared city glittered with color, its myriad facets fragmenting a yellower sun's light in prismatic patterns. Its inhabitants lived and pulsed, strode, took their ease, in a panoply of light and shadow. Humanity and outworlders coursed through the markets, entertainment plazas, malls, arcades. Pleasure boats cut the lake waters, plasteen sails reflecting, shimmering. None saw themselves as the ghosts they would be to Terrans of fifty millennia ahead.

Damon and Kira strode among them, feeling the press of mind and body. As a concession to this urban scene, and because it sometimes pleased herself and Damon, Kira had taken on a humaniform persona. Her arm was cool on his, the light hair glinting gold against tan in the late day sun.

Cardeen Mar made room for them at his umbrellaed table off the esplanade. He rose to hold Kira's chair for her. Or was it to show off his silk and satin finery? His hose outlined a well-turned Tudor leg.

Kira ordered cider, Damon a scotch and soda, which he had programmed the tavern's computer to concoct. The drink was enjoying a vogue of some staying power. Cardeen stayed in character: he favored ale.

"What news on the Rialto?" Cardeen inquired.

Damon sighed. He was to blame for this craze as well.

"Our scientists have settled in. They're rattling around the visitors' apartments and getting itchy."

"Can we expect them inside, Damon? We could do with some outside excitement."

Damon looked at Kira, who answered for them both.

"Too disruptive. They have a lot of learning to do before they're turned loose on such cosmopolitan dream shatterers as you, Cardeen. You'd find them rough and sharp-edged.''

Cardeen chuckled. He was carrying the persona of an Elizabethan dandy, silken doublet and silken cape in hues of green and gold.

"Sharp-edged indeed. I'd like to talk poetry with Vijay Chaudhuri.''

"And Malcolm Gant would love to get your brain on *his* chopping block. Hack it to pieces, centrifuge it. Whatever it takes to find out what makes it tick.''

Cardeen toyed with his fruit tart, his long fingers manipulating a two-tined fork in graceful arcs. His lower consciousness spun a pattern of eating as art form. Damon's table manners would seem vulgar, a tavern bravo's by comparison.

"Would the Council deny them the city and we them for their whole stay? Must we know them only by proxy?''

Kira tossed her tawny hair in impatience.

"They'd be disruptive, Cardeen. They're not ready. Stop letting this foppish pose addle your brain. They've got learning to do before they parade for your entertainment.''

Cardeen took the reproach well. He responded not angrily, but with a genuine wistfulness.

"It's more than that, you know, Kira. Damon and his Shakespeare, his Sidney, his Marlowe have been a great inspiration. I haven't been this productive in millennia. I'd like to converse with the poet. Who knows what would come of it?"

Kira acquiesced. "If it would give us sonnets like in your last quarto, it might be worth it. But it can be done without allowing them the city."

The multicolored crowds poured by their table, a torrent to their eddying pool. Some were on their way to the theatre across the plaza where Cardeen Mar's tragedy was playing. Cast in Shakespearean form, it had perhaps transcended it. Perhaps, so it seemed to Damon. He lacked the cultural awareness to appreciate some of the local nuances. He lacked the multilevel perception to see beyond the tracings of some of its intricacies. But he could value the poetry.

He hoped that Vijay Chaudhuri, at least, would be allowed in.

The commons room of the visitors' wing was large and open. It could accommodate many more visitors than the five here, and certainly had. Not all of them had been human. The fluid plasticity of the furniture attested to that. So did the scale and amenities of several of the apartments.

The outer wall was completely transparent, opening to a lakeside vista and forest beyond. The Terrans gravitated to a grouping of chairs and tables near that wall, putting the forbidding expanse of a large common hall behind them and out of sight.

"When do we meet the natives?" Kerry Burns asked.

"You've met Kira, here," Damon said. Kira looked up from her place on the floor, head erect, ears alert. "She and Harrod Dan were all I met for quite a while."

"And why was that?" Stenmark asked, propelling his sled to a drink dispenser.

"Most of the humans—I mean the first generation ones, the ones like you and me, though not quite—they're exploring their world through new eyes. They've got enough wonders to work through: their past culture and its hundreds of thousands of years, many layers of complexities. They've got one lifetime to enjoy this aspect of the human condition, as do we—but they're more intent on making use of it. We're not too interesting to them, with our jejune ways, our buzzing questions. They're too busy enjoying, or trying to learn and answer questions of their own."

"But, damn it, that's the only way I can study a culture—by observing! Okay—and asking questions."

"Poor Kerry," Chabron rumbled, his dark eyes glinting. "Margaret Mead to these non-Samoans you cannot be."

"Can it, Roger. You don't know anything about my field. It's come a far longer way. It's Damon's field, too. He knows."

"Yes, I do," Damon said, looking beyond her to the lake, seeing from memory what she could only imagine: people on that lake, an aspect of the culture that she sought. "But even you can do with some solid background learning before you plunge in. You're getting that at this library. And you're in deep enough so that you're getting an actual dialogue with your local analogs."

"Canned dialogue. Programmed answers, if I stumble onto the right cues."

Damon started to contradict her. Kira signaled a block and Damon backed off.

"It's all right for Roger here," Kerry went on. "All he cares about is getting deeper into that computer for its own sake. He doesn't care about people."

"You know better, my dear Kerry."

"I'm not talking about screwing, Roger. Give up on that—at least as far as I'm concerned. I mean meaningful interchange."

"I didn't know that one precluded the other," Malcolm Gant said dryly.

Perhaps our guests are right, Kira responded so that all could understand. *What kind of contact would each of you like? Roger?*

"I hardly know. I lack the data to adequately respond."

Kerry snorted.

Kerry?

"To walk and talk among a community. That's all."

We can arrange that. Vijay?

"Like Roger, it is not a question of other people. For different reasons. He has his computer. I have the literature. But, perhaps, to speak to a living poet? One would be enough."

That shall be done. Mac?

"To observe a mind transfer. To have access to the surgeon. To feel what happens."

You may not yet be ready. You still view it as a surgical procedure, which is only partially the truth. Yours is a complex field, and you have been here only a month. But perhaps we'll try anyway. That I cannot answer for now. But I shall ask. Dr. Stenmark?

"To visit with any who care to visit with me."

A more catholic, open view. I had expected a more elitist preference, considering your professional stature. I think, Dr. Stenmark, that even among our disinterested people, there will be many to accept that offer.

Kira stood up and stretched her spine, her rear legs splayed out stiffly as she arched her back.

I think you, too, Kerry, are ready to participate in our culture as well as observe. There was real amusement there. *Damon will explain—in time.*

Kerry noted that Damon was reddening visibly as he and Kira withdrew.

*　　*　　*

Surgery was still surgery—in some respects. Malcolm Gant found the setting familiar. Before him on a table was the patient, or one of them. A man in his later years, sinewy and brown of skin, looked up at Gant and Dessin Tev with interested eyes. His head was depilated and his skull gleamed white. He seemed quite at ease on the table—platform, really—which molded to his body and cocooned him in its depths.

"Comfortable, Gorman?" the surgeon asked.

"More so than I remember for some time. Your table makes it hard to say farewell to the body it supports."

Dessin Tev laughed, as any doctor would at his patient's operating room jests, no matter how labored. He took Gant by the arm to another platform, where a deerlike animal lay, apparently sedated.

"Gorman's new body. Of course it need not be here, as there'll be no direct transfer. Could just as well be a continent away."

"Why here, then?" Gant asked.

"Economy of labor. I can just as well monitor two receptacles as one. Saves having to have someone else, an analog of myself, elsewhere. We don't need many surgeons, you know. So we don't have them."

That was a difference. Dessin Tev didn't seem to be the nexus that a Terran neurosurgeon would be in such a procedure.

"No, of course not." Dessin Tev laughed again, enjoying this jest and its implications at least as much as that of his patient. "We're just the handmaidens here. Surely you can sense the others."

Gant could. He couldn't put definition to it; the presences about him were inchoate, beyond his ken in their deepest essences. But he could feel the psychic roils and currents.

"They're real, all right. They're out-of-body. Some of them are in the computer, using that as a base matrix. And that's where Gorman's going as a way station to this transfer. They'll take him there."

"That's why his new body doesn't have to be here?"

"That's right. Gorman prefers to end up in this vicinity, though; this is where his friends are. More importantly, he's not mastered the out-of-body state. We want him warehoused in the computer matrix— think of it as a timeless safe harbor—so there's no chance of losing him en route. And *that's* why we're here."

Despite his recent education, Gant still found aspects of this puzzling. He had to admit as well that his ego found the lesser role of his medical counterpart deflating.

"Think of us as *banderilleros*," Dessin Tev had told him earlier. Dessin had become a recent Hemingway aficionado. "We're not the center of attraction. The matador is. The bull is. The analogy holds

lso in what we do. We're going to plant the probes,
he terminals, into those two brains, just as a
anderillero delivers his implants.''

"Why is that necessary?" Gant had asked.

"Because we want a real transfer. Gorman has
mited psi skills and can't do it himself. Of course,
e could easily scan Gorman's brain and recreate it
1 the computer, then transfer off that template—
nprint or overlay it on the host cortex. You'd have a
jorman analog, but not Gorman. He'd be gone.
hat's why we don't put people through matter trans-
er. But we're going to lead Gorman right out of his
rain in a partly physical transfer, into the computer,
1en into his new home. He'll know it, and we'll
now it. You might catch a part of it.''

Gant felt that he was looking millennia ahead in
1edical procedure, yet retrograded as far in his com-
1unications. He felt he was in a Socratic dialogue.
'here was a certain whimsy to this, and he continued.

"Gorman's essence—his soul, then—is translat-
ble into electrical impulses?''

"In a way. Part of Gorman will follow along a
euro-conductive path. Part will follow along in par-
llel but outside.''

"I'm most interested in where you implant the
lectrode—where some could hold the soul resides.''

Dessin Tev was seemingly being paid in amuse-
1ent. He laughed again. "Nothing that simple—or
1etaphysical. We're stimulating the temporal lobes,

triggering off memories. That's a good part of the essence of Gorman Nel. Or anyone. Simultaneously, we've introduced into the host cortex large doses of the enzyme produced from cloning a culture containing a fragment of the host's copy DNA in plasmid wrappings—obtained through reverse transcriptase— the enzyme that facilitates the laying down of memories, forging the new nerve chains. At the same time, we're stimulating the host hippocampus to help imprint those memories on the blank cortex."

Dessin Tev paused. "Of course, Gorman won't see it in those terms. Rightly, because that's just the physiology of it. He'll be consciously working down the neural chain of Gorman-to-computer-to-new-cortex, reliving his old memories and implanting them as new ones. He'll have help—a linkage that's partly the minds of others. Between his efforts and the shepherding of those others, we'll get him to his new home."

Gant watched the implantation of the *banderillas*. He wished he could avoid seeing things in that light, but the imagery had stuck. Dessin Tev was lost to him. He was inside Gorman, feeling the texture of his essence, comforting and sedating. Others were there, too, urging, guiding, and assisting Gorman Nel. Gorman Nel's body was dying. Like a drowning sailor, Gorman had to free himself from his body, plunging toward the bottom like a torpedoed vessel.

If Gorman didn't free himself, he would die and be gone forever.

Much of this was beyond Malcolm Gant experientially. And he vaguely resented the limited role of his medical counterpart in the process. But he wondered, feeling the strength, the gentleness, the patience, the power around him. Its aura imprinted on Gant's brain as Gorman Nel's left his body to journey to the forest animal beside him. Tomorrow Gorman Nel would be bounding through wooded glens and valleys.

Two steps beyond the entry portal, face left and get it right between the eyes.

Damon blinked. There was no human substance here. He was looking at a wall hanging, artfully hung and posed—a Lydian Council robe of ancient days. Its flowing lines focused to the sunburst orange nova of a speaker serving notice of a major oration or policy proposal, something beyond everyday legislative routine. Seldom worn in its fashionable heyday of millennia ago, and never now. Certainly never hung as ornamentation.

A lot of impact there. It must have raised the eyebrows of more than one visitor. Damon raised his, now.

"I wove it myself from a graphic at the library," Kerry tossed out, as she ordered from the drink dispenser. Damon looked about the rest of her apartment, its concave walls with their abstract imprintings, Kerry's unusual furniture groupings—including a loom with material in progress. "Checked first to see if there were any taboos against it."

"As any good anthropologist should. But if there are any taboos here at all, I've yet to find one—and I've been at it longer than you."

"It's produced results, though, I can tell you that."

"An interesting professional technique. But what results, what reactions? Shock? Amusement?"

"Perhaps. But also interest, maybe admiration for my innovation. Or audacity."

Damon nodded. "You may be right. You have my interest and admiration. Along with the amusement."

Kerry laughed and crossed the room to the guest couch where Damon had settled, extending his drink.

"Weaving," Damon went on. "That how you spend your spare time?"

"Part of it. Any other suggestions?"

"Your psi exercises. Thought about that when you picked up on my interest in the wall hanging. Or was it my eye motion?"

"Maybe both. Does it matter?"

Damon looked at Kerry, keeping his features neutral. He projected exasperation. Kerry blinked.

"Better. Glad you got that. Nuance and feeling are something at least. But get on to words. You need that precision if you want to understand these people. And I gather you do. It may be peripheral to Gant's and Chabron's fields, but it's supposed to be your main professional interest.''

It was Kerry's turn to think. And to look exasperated. Her brow furrowed and her lips tightened. ''The locals don't seem to care overly.''

''Of course they don't. They see a limited point. The Once Born are full of the newness of it all and wrapped up in developing their psi powers so they don't go down with their bodies at the end. The Kindred—sea, forest, air—they can't communicate verbally and since you can't read them, *they* have to project on *you*. That's tiring. And to what end?''

''Knowledge. Some of them seem quite dedicated to it.''

''Sure. *Their* knowledge. What do they care, beyond a moment's eyeblink, of the knowledge enhancement of a farflung, lesser developed culture? Or its representatives in the here and now? They care about educating us only to the point where we don't misapprehend them and blunder into culture-threatening confrontations with them and other sentient races. They'll help us grow up but we've got to sharpen our basic tools so as to make it something better than a trudge through the swamp for them. That's why I'm telling you to work harder at your psi exercises.''

Kerry had never sat down, but was pacing the room with the restlessness of a cheetah. Lithe, slim, wiry, she exuded caged animal tension. Damon took her restless form in his consciousness, extended her helmet of coppery hair to a lengthening pelt that reached and extended in glacierlike progress past her nape and over her body, her clothes melting away to nothingness. Her fingernails extended to curved and lethal claws. He lengthened her forearms, then dropped her to all fours, swung her around to face him challengingly over her shoulder. Damon held the image, let it hang unshielded—but also unprojected.

"Good Lord! Is that how you see me?"

Damon superimposed his own image, also feral and feline-adapted, approaching and then mounting Kerry's arced and accommodating form.

"Oh, yes! Can we do it like that?"

Damon looked across at her, dissolved back to her true form. She was flushed. So was he. A vein pulsed in her tanned throat, her sinews taut around it. He was hard as a quarterstaff. He sensed her genital wetness without probing. She was projecting.

"Some of the positive fallout from doing your exercises." He held out his hand as she knelt by the couch.

"You're making me a believer." She put down her drink and unbuttoned her blouse slowly. Damon looked appreciatively at the hard, erect nipples. He reached out to hold, then roll one between thumb and forefinger. Then he projected her small breasts flattening to feline litheness. Once again, her hair lengthened to body pelt and she moved forward to meet him.

* * *

"I *am* a believer." Kerry stretched lazily, her fingers curved inward. Even without Damon's input she was maintaining a quasi-feline persona.

"Lots of possibilities for the initiated," Damon said. "Triads, quads. And I don't mean group sex, though that can be a part of it. There's sharing and imprinting on a whole range of levels. But you've got to have something to offer beyond novelty."

"Do I?"

"Sure, but not the tools. Or just the rudimentary ones. I'll help you develop them. You're ready for a quantum leap, but you'll need a boost—the same kind I got—if you're to do it before you leave. You've got barely a year to do it."

She looked at him crosswise, then stretched up and strode fluidly across the room. Kerry liked to think on the prowl. On the way she picked up her blouse and shrugged it on, leaving it unbuttoned. She turned back to Damon on the couch and walked toward him with that head-on look he liked about her. Even after satiety, her flat belly and prominent, still wet pubic tuft excited him sensually.

"You're leaving, too, aren't you?" she challenged.

"Yes—but I want you further along by that time."

"More than a believer? An acolyte?"

"Let's not push it too far. An ally, perhaps. But at least a spirit with independent strength. Concealed strength, too. You may need it."

Her brow furrowed. "You mean Gant?"

"There'll always be Gants. And more powerful Gants behind him. I've learned that; that learning process is what's kept me here. Besides, Gant's only the short-term problem—though well on the way to being part of the long-term one. He's got ambitions and drives he can never satisfy here, and he's shown no inclination to modify them." Damon paused. "And I'll tell you another. Gant works *hard* at his psi exercises. And he digs for the principles behind them. Even without direction he's coming off a stronger base of powers and knowledge of those powers than any of the rest of you."

"I'll believe Gant," Kerry said. "I don't think Roger works at it at all. He's more interested in getting into the computer. And Dr. Stenmark—no one sees him. He's into his world of theoretical physics, I'd guess."

"You're right about Chabron. He's discovered early on that he has very little psi ability. It's not an evenly distributed gift, you know. But Dr. Stenmark works as hard as Gant. He's got a motivation. He wants to stay."

Kerry shot Damon an interrogatory with a conceptual visual overlay. He shook his head. "No, he'd never be far enough along to join the Kindred. And he's even further away from reaching the out-of-body state. He'd never make it before his own body gave out—if he had to work within the confines of real time.''

"How can he get around that?''

Damon rose from the guest couch. He strode to the view wall and looked out and up, through the lattice-work of leaves, their green lightened by the sunlight filtering through. He turned back to Kerry.

"Catechism time. Okay. You know by now that the impression of this society that the first expedition got—had given to them—was true, as far as it went. Quite simplistic, though. Give me an encapsulation of this society as you've dug it out. Then I'll do what they won't do here.'' He smiled wryly. "Give your data gratuitously.''

"That would be a novelty, all right. How basic do you want it?''

"Basic. Give me an Anthropology One overview.''

Kerry took a breath and resumed her pacing. Probably how she lectured as well as how she did her thinking. Not open-bloused and bare-assed, though.

Kerry broke her stride and turned to face him, hand on hip and laughing.

"Jesus! Let me think!''

"You caught that one.''

"Thank God I couldn't read when I was lecturing at the university. If that's what my students were projecting, I'd never finish a lecture.''

Damon grinned. "Hey, teach—you're the one show-ing the dirty pictures.''

"Dammit, get your cock down, then—if it's a lecture you really want."

"I'll try. Start talking."

Kerry went to the wardrobe and came back wearing shorts, her shirt buttoned. Damon took it in with mixed feelings.

"Okay—Lydian society. The Once Borns. Close genetically to you and me, but with a knowledge and certainty of lives and consciousness to come—if they develop their psi powers sufficiently to cut loose from their bodies before their bodies do them in. A certain carelessness in other matters, almost a conscious indulgence in childhood beyond the body's childhood parameters. The minimizing of responsibilities to the basic: maintaining the city and physical plant, raising food they don't want machine-produced, bringing up—but not necessarily doing all of the educating—of the children. They can, of course, handle serious matters seriously when that's called for."

Kerry looked at Damon for reassurance, the lecturer seeking confirmation from her audience.

"You're right. That's the Once Born, and that's enough on them. They're just the tip of the iceberg."

"The Kindred," Kerry continued. "Next step beyond. A way station to some, a dead end to others. Life extension in a highly specialized way. Free spirits, some Thinkers. The Thinkers seem to be theoretically inclined, divorced from the workaday world and policy making. Whatever policy *has* to be made, short of infrequent off-world visitations. Most of the Kindred are sensualists, some of the highest sort. Others are back-to-nature types in the truest sense. They're all working in varying degrees toward reaching out-of-body capability. It's that or die.''

She paused again.

''I do think I'm missing something, but I'm not sure what. I'll sum up the Kindred by calling them a necessary but transitory middle stage toward out-of-body.''

''You're off there, I'm afraid,'' Damon said. ''The Kindred are a visible but also small tip of the iceberg. They're not a necessary middle station. They're a wild offshoot, a very minority cult. But not without their place, even to those who have little use for their way, who dislike their breeding and use of animals for their cortex. Don't let me sidetrack you, though. Keep going.''

''The Out of Body. I'm on less firm ground here. By definition, I can't observe. I've felt their presence, though. Enough to believe from experience as well as on faith. Some of them are essences temporarily loosed from their bodies of flesh. Some have gone beyond, their bodies themselves gone and history. At times they're quite removed from temporal affairs; at other times they seem to be the true guiding, caretaking force. They seem to be here, attached to this gravitational field, so to speak. Or maybe they're everywhere, maybe even everywhen. I don't know.''

"I can't tell you either," Damon admitted. "Not on that last point. There are several stages, not all of which I can conceptually fathom. I think Dr. Stenmark will be able to, if he makes it. But that's another sidetrack. Got any more?''

"There seems to be an out-of-body state completely divorced from physical and temporal restraints, to which everyone ultimately aspires. Beyond further contact with us. Close to some concepts of nirvana. There are lots of parallels to the Buddhist Wheel of Life, as even Vijay—who's no anthropologist—has observed. I think he's confounded, though, to find rebirth within the body of an animal to be a developmental step up and away from the Wheel rather than one backward.''

She took a deep breath and sat back into a host chair, tossing her coppery hair. Back to him.

"You've got three quarters of the mosaic, most of it right. Very good on the Out of Body, particularly since a lot of that's pure induction. But you've missed on the Kindred. The actual middle link between Once Born and Out of Body—for those who need or *want* the link, and some don't—are the computer worlds. And to some, *that* is the end state, by choice or lack of capability to make it to Out of Body. Some just don't want to cut loose. The computer works as their base, their body. Well over 99.9 percent—to several decimal places, actually—of this world's currently sentient beings reside in the computer worlds. And there are millions of worlds, on slow time, fast time. Most of their inhabitants will never leave. Some use the Kindred as their senses and mind link to our real, now-time world, trading links to theirs. And they can tailor their worlds anyway they want. There are pleasure worlds, offworlds, fantasy and dream worlds, literal thinktanks—you name it.''

Kerry was leaning forward, excited and flushed in a newer way.

''Can you take me in?''

''Perhaps. Kira took me in initially. You'll need a physical hookup, an actual conduit to the computer. It takes out-of-body capability of a degree to do it otherwise—and you're a long way from that.''

''And you?''

''Not so far.''

''Have any of the others been in?''

''Stenmark has. He's doing his psi work in a very slow-time world. He has to compress time and at least develop the capability to make it to computer residency before we leave or before his body breaks down. He really *wants* the freedom from bodily constraints on pure thought. The Council has decided to allow him to stay. Gant, now—he may have guessed from his work in the surgery. He knows that the computer is a holding tank in the Kindred transplant, and he may suspect more. Chabron, too—though that's not his area of interest. In learning about what makes the computer tick, he may stumble on the concept.''

''How about Vijay?''

''Besides Stenmark, he's the only one the Lydians want in. All we really have to offer them are our arts. And that's all they want. I fed them the contents of the *Fairbairn*'s library—music, too—and that's been an ongoing interest in a lot of their worlds. An outright craze in some. Trouble is, Vijay's not very psi gifted. We're working on him and at least letting him talk with those inside. He doesn't know they're inside, of course.''

Kerry walked over to the view wall, her turn to stand looking out, focusing long. She turned to Damon.

''This is exciting stuff.''

''A lot of today has been exciting stuff.''

''This is a different kind of exciting,'' she said, coming back. ''I want to think about it.''

''Now?''

She opened her waistband and stepped out of her shorts.

''Later.''

''You're a hard man to see, Dr. Stenmark.'' Malcolm Gant was visibly annoyed. ''Even harder to see alone.''

''Mr. Hart is not here on his own initiative, Dr.

Gant. I've asked him to attend this meeting. Out of genuine concern, I'm sorry to admit.'' Stenmark's voice crackled with asperity. "Of course I could have asked one of our hosts, but I thought better of putting this lot of linen on show."

"Did you really expect strong-arm methods, Dr. Stenmark? From your personal physician? I kept you alive on the trip out."

"Dr. Gant, I've learned to fear zeal, no matter how well-intentioned. But I do feel I owe you, or whom you represent, a hearing and perhaps a bit more. Both of these you'll get. And I'll point out that you're not now my personal physician, and never were by choice."

Malcolm Gant shifted uncomfortably in his chair. This study room of the library—neutral ground— housed a collection of old art folios, bound and shelved along an entire wall behind. They seemed to overhang Gant, brooding and heavy in their ancient and oversize slipcases.

"To the point, Dr. Stenmark. I hear that you've been offered residence here and plan to accept it. I must ask you to reconsider."

Stenmark regarded the doctor with ill-disguised contempt.

"I won't ask you on what authority you make such a meddlesome request, because I really do not care. I shall simply tell you that I am an old man, close to dying. That I can accept. I did not ask for residence;

it was offered. But it is not to continue a tiresome bodily existence that I cling. It is the chance *to continue with my work!* To study. To *learn.* Among congenial spirits and on the very highest plane of inquiry! And now, what countervailing claims can you advance to dissuade me?''

Gant continued his uncomfortable fidgeting, but pressed on nonetheless. ''Loyalty. To your world. For the opportunity given you to *get* here to do your work.''

''You shall have my journal, Dr. Gant. There are enough new avenues of investigation, sufficient advances on current theory to keep a hundred physicists busy and happy for years. My passage will have been paid.''

Gant, no matter his discomfort, had been restraining his innermost feelings behind an impenetrable barricade of psi shielding. Apparently much of his exercises had gone toward that, a tribute to his fortress mentality. Now Gant dropped his shield, freely allowing—projecting—his feelings of rage and frustration. Damon looked on in despair and Stenmark actually recoiled.

''Loyalty!'' Gant's rage was cold and controlled, channeled outward. Damon did his best to damp the savage flow, throwing back at Gant his professed disdain of strong-arm methods. Gant pressed on. ''Dr. Stenmark—don't you recognize loyalty?''

Damon rose and moved to Stenmark's sled control. With a trembling hand, the physicist waved him back, but looked to him to speak.

Damon turned back to face across the table. "Believe me, Gant, I've done this scene before. Dr. Stenmark and I do recognize the pull of loyalty. As always, it is its object that is in question."

Dr. Stenmark nodded his agreement and reached for his motive controls. Damon stood between Stenmark and Gant, who had risen from his chair and stood leaning on the conference table, hands splayed out before him.

Dr. Stenmark pushed through the doorway. Damon followed behind, turned, and closed the door.

A soft, southerly gust took the waves to the brink of whitecaps, bellied the sails of pleasure craft and windrunners. On the party boats long hair curled back from sun-warmed faces or whipped out before them. Ruffled sleeves of silk and loose-fitting skirts of gossamer billowed to fullness.

Kerry raised her glass delightedly, catching the sun in its claret depths. Around her, music bounced and lilted off the crystal filigree of the ship's fittings, resonating in deeper tones from its crystal hull. She felt herself floating on transparency, flying before any chance breeze.

"It's wonderful! I love it! Why must we leave?"

"We don't have to, but we've been on the lake two hours. I'd like to show you the city. Even that could wait. But now—this day—there are some people who won't. Not these. I promise, you'll want very much to meet them.''

Kerry nodded and Damon put the tiller over. They pointed toward the city, multifaceted and prismatic, soaring before them on the far lakeshore. They drew nearer and Kerry could pick out motion: craft hovering about its landing stages, lifts rising and descending in transparent shafts, banners and gonfalons snapping from poles on terraces of greenery. Damon put the craft on lift and they planed upward on a gradual slope till the city became their total vision.

''Is it fantasy?''

''No. It's a true re-creation, though something of a composite. It's the city in its heyday, forty to sixty thousand years ago. You'll see some Terran influence, though of course that never was. This cycle, it's mostly Elizabethan.''

''I thought I recognized the music. Are the people real? Even the outworlders?''

''Yes indeed. No need for simulacra here. This is one of the most popular worlds. Even with the outworlders who've been granted residence here. Some of them are from races now extinct. Novas mostly, some suicidally self-generated.''

''That's sad. Not today on that, Damon.'' She held tight to his arm as they stood on the central landing stage and watched the colorful parade flow by.

Damon took her on the walkways, choosing the route to sample bazaars, open-air music shells, the Teardrop Gallery, the Stair of Souls. Their mood changed several times in their passage, from delight to contemplative withdrawal to awe and at last to frolic. It was an artfully chosen route that had introduced Damon to the city periods before.

Beneath a shady parasol a place was waiting at a full and gaily-decked table. Kerry clutched his arm even more tightly.

"It's Vijay! Is it his first time, too?"

Damon nodded.

"Who's that with him? Is that who brought him in?"

Vijay rose as they approached, a study in white, deep brown, black. The woman beside him rose, too. Slender, lithe, in almost transparent gossamer set off with bright satin streamers. High-breasted, hair of fine gold, open and upturned eyes.

"Vijay!" Kerry took both his hands and looked into his face, then to the woman. "Would you introduce me?"

"Must he?" The woman smiled.

"Reach out a little," Damon prodded.

Kerry took a puzzled step back, then forward to touch a hand.

"Kira?" A tear ran down Kerry's cheek, but she kept her gaze resolutely forward. "Kira—you're so beautiful!"

You too, Kerry. Don't doubt it.

Later Kerry would not remember who had thought those words—Damon? Vijay? Kira? Perhaps all three.

Damon pulled out a chair for Kerry and gestured playfully. "Let the festivities begin!"

It became a time of coming out and of paying court. Glasses were raised, toasts offered freely. A parade of visitors pressed forward to introduce themselves, talk, glitter, and move on.

Cardeen Mar approached, resplendent in satin and velvet. Nodding to Damon, he bowed to Kerry and pressed her hand.

" 'More lovely and more temperate than a summer's day.' " Then, turning, "And Kira— 'A very riband in the cap of youth.' "

Kira laughed appreciatively, but rolled her eyes.

It was Vijay, though, whom Cardeen took aside for extended conversation.

There were many others to take Cardeen's place.

Luncheon followed, hardly tasted. Conversation and spectacle dominated. Cardeen took them across the plaza to his play, a very creditable effort, all agreed. "But not up to Shakespearean standards," Cardeen admitted. "That's why we venerate him, after all. But Jonson I'll accept."

Then back again to their table for pastries, more talk, and drinks.

"I'll say it." Kerry put her head to Damon's

shoulder. "I'm talked and toasted out. Still—must it end?"

"What better time? Let's finish as we began, with a sail on the lake. The city is splendid with the sun setting behind it."

"Still—nighttime in the city!"

"Next time." Damon raised her to her feet for the farewell toast.

"A request for next time, Damon." Kerry's thought came shyly, held back and unspoken till they were again on the water. " 'A summer's day' is well enough—but can I be a 'riband in the cap of youth'?"

"You can if you want. You'll have to let me—or someone, maybe Kira—in to help you. You can't yet mold that persona by yourself."

"There's a danger." She drew back. "You'd see me again later as I am now."

"And want you just as much. It's not a comparison, you know. Your image becomes a meld, a totality when you let a lover in."

"A last question. Has Kira been your lover?"

"Of course. She was my first one here."

"I like that." Again she gripped his arm, turning from the shimmering water and the city now far away. "Let's go back now. And let's make love. Not lust. Love."

"Vijay, I know that Mac Gant's been hassling Dr. Stenmark about his residency decision. I'll ask you a brief question, and I'll back off if you want. Has he been pressuring you, and do you need help?''

Vijay Chaudhuri regarded Damon from behind old-fashioned spectacles. A gentle look, and not at all worldly wise. So it seemed. So different from Rachman Khan Pindharee, as was to be expected. Same land; different cultures. And different persons. One always had to allow for that.

"Mac did speak to me, Damon. I don't mind talking about it. He asked me if I had been offered residency, and did I plan to accept it." Vijay smiled slightly. "Like yours, actually two questions."

A little harmless indulgence there, a bit of professional precision. Vijay went on. "I told him that no offer had been made and likely never would. I had made it clear to our hosts that I seek release from the Wheel in my culture's way. I don't mind sharpening my psi abilities—what few I have. That could be reasonably considered an extension of right mindfulness, part of the eightfold path. But I planned no extension of life through actual psychic transfer.''

"Not even to the out-of-body state?"

"But, of course, being a semanticist as well as a Hinayana Buddhist, that could be considered one conception of the state of nirvana. That is a philosophical point as well as one of semantics.''

Damon shook his head in admiration.

"Dr. Gant shook his head, too, when I made that point to him," Vijay said with a mischievous smile

"I think his head shake was one of frustration," Damon said.

"I think so. But then, that was my aim."

Damon felt a wave of feeling for this man. It must have been difficult for him in so many ways. With his reverence for all life, it would pain him to live among the Kindred, who bred and blanked out young animal cortex to accept their imprint. Humane though it was, no matter how greater the number of other lives saved by doing it this ecologically efficient way—did the end justify the near-term deprivation of life? To Vijay, it likely did not. Nor to others of the race—many of them—who held the Kindred way in disregard. Better the computer worlds. But even they could be no permanent refuge for a man of Vijay's beliefs.

Damon resolved to spend some time boosting Vijay's meager abilities. If it gave Vijay a leg up on becoming a *bhodisattva,* so much better. Perhaps a little good karma might fall out Damon's way.

Damon shook his head in admiration once again. This time the admiration was of the grudging sort.

Before him, electrodes on head within the scanner unit, lay the supine form of Malcolm Gant, M.D. and adventurer. A bold and surprising aspect of personality. Nearby, and at the surgery's main computer terminal, sat Roger Chabron, looking not at all bold. He looked completely lost and fearful of getting up from the familiarity of the computer bank lest he lose all hope of ever finding his way to safety. He looked fearful of Damon and Kira as well.

"It's okay, Roger. No one's going to come down on you. We respect the effort and the daring."

Even if it makes for awkward consequences. That from Kira, beyond Chabron's limited threshold of reception.

"When is Mac coming back?" Chabron asked nervously. He eyed Kira as if he once again saw her as the forest predator she had appeared at first contact. Specifically, as if she were about to take a bite—and more—out of varied parts of his hide.

"When he wants to. Or when we get him. What's the matter—didn't he tell you what he was up to?"

Chabron was showing all the uneasiness of a man discovering that he had been used. That must have been almost as bad to a prideful Frenchman as being cuckolded. Perpetrators of different sex; same embarrassment. He squirmed miserably in his chair and offered up his explanations grudgingly. "He said he was going into the computer. I gave him the access I had achieved so far. I've been teaching him some computer theory and language and paths. Is that bad?"

"You must think so. Didn't he tell you what he expected to find?"

"He said only that he wanted to explore its intelligence. He said that he knew it functioned as a holding tank during Kindred transfers. He wanted to see what it was to live within the computer."

Well, perhaps Roger believed that. Perhaps Gant did. Damon rather doubted it, but didn't care enough to probe.

"He did the brain scan and the conduit positioning himself?"

Chabron nodded.

Damon turned to Kira. They started for the door.

"Where are you going?" Chabron was half rising from his seat of sanctuary, evidently fearing being left alone more than being inquisitioned.

Damon tossed it over his shoulder: "To get him out, Roger."

Away from Chabron, in an adjoining cubicle, Damon and Kira reclined on resting pads and went out-of-body and into the computer through the psi terminal.

Over to Gant's access route, Kira indicated. *We can use the monitor to backtrack his path.*

Gant had tried several side excursions, including a hell world that had probably scared the hell out of him. Though maybe not. He had that tough mental shielding, a form probably unfamiliar to the denizens there. He had seemingly gotten out before they had penetrated it. Eventually he had picked the most traveled route, the one leading to the city.

Nighttime there. They found him in a jewel box off the main esplanade, entranced by the musical resonances bouncing off its interior crystal facets, light sparkling in symphony. They backed out and waited till Gant emerged in his own time, bemused and flying high.

Damon and Kira flanked him from behind as he gawked at the colorful parade striding and being carried down the midway.

"Howdy, Cousin." Damon took one arm; Kira, in her Once Born persona, took the other. "Welcome to the Big City."

"And well done," Kira said.

Gant had no trouble recognizing Kira from her mental texture. Recognition was not his concern. "No hard feelings?"

"Not at all," Damon said. "Most of these worlds are open to any who can make it in. Of course, not all here may choose to traffic with you. But that's true to some degree for all tourists."

"And there'll be some closed to you for other reasons," Kira added. "Mainly the slow-time ones. We'll help you—it's handy to have a guide to steer you to the more congenial worlds."

Gant shuddered. "I don't care if I don't see one certain world again. You can close that to me any time."

Kira laughed. "The hell worlds are open to all.

It's up to you to do the avoiding and abstaining. But no need to abstain here. Can we buy you a drink? Maybe give you a few tips? Then we'll turn you loose again."

"I'll take that drink, and then maybe I'm ready to go back. I've had enough for one time." He eyed them warily. "So long as I can return."

"We really *do* mean it, Mac," Kira reassured him. "Just obey the interdictions. They'll be enforced anyway. Be a good citizen and you're welcome."

"Don't *always* push for an adversary confrontation," Damon added his own emphasis. "It doesn't have to be, unless you press it."

"Let's get that drink," Gant responded.

They moved off into the sparkling, shattering city night.

"Do I have it right?" Kerry asked. "We do it 'in the privacy of our own home,' so to speak? There's no special room or place for it?"

"Come off it, Kerry," Damon said. "You know this isn't an orgy. It's not a voyeuristic thing either. It's a sharing. But if you're uncomfortable with it, let's not."

Kerry walked across the room—her room—as usual, doing her thinking and arguing on the prowl. It wouldn't be her room for long. The ship would land tomorrow, and they'd be gone the same day. Leaving. It always came to that. To some the prime focus was in where they were going. Damon envied the anticipation but not the renunciation. Leaving was easy when the next destination always looked greener. Could anything have looked greener than the memories of home when Damon had walked away from the *Fairbairn* those many years ago? Could anything look greener than this world which he was now leaving?

He wanted this congress, union, melding. If it came to it, he wanted Kira more than Kerry, this night in particular. He made certain that Kerry didn't glimpse that tilt. Kira knew. She was too skilled not to. She was also too tactful to touch on it openly.

With departure imminent, Kerry's apartment had lost most of its individuality. The wall hangings were gone—that wonderful robe replication in particular—packed away to take home. Damon had lost one early fear—that Kerry would display it openly, like a South Seas voyager displaying his tikis and masks to any casual visitor. Familiarity had bred respect.

"You're right. I know that this union with Kira and Maldir would be an intimacy, not a bestiality. And I think I really love Kira. I don't know Maldir well, but I trust Kira's judgment. And I trust you. Maybe love you, too."

"It hasn't been *all* bestiality with us, then? I'm glad."

Kerry laughed lightly and her prowl eased into an ambulatory meditation.

"Damn—you know what I mean. I *am* a private person, even if sometimes an abandoned one. Well should you know *that*. I may open up others, but I don't open easily to them."

Damon walked over to the wicker table beside the guest couch and picked up the decanter and two glasses. Drink dispensers were more utilitarian, but function carried low priority at the moment. He poured the wine judiciously, taking time to admire the ruddy color—flashing unexpectedly back to a set of ancient pharmaceutical bottles filled with ruby, emerald, Tyrian purple, that had once fascinated him in an Earthside antique shop. Home memories were beginning to flood back, tempering the pain of leaving.

"Of course, I could look at this as an anthropological field trip. . . ."

"Don't," Damon cut her short, striding toward her and extending the long-stemmed wine glass. As she reached for it he took her hand and held it with both of his wrapped around the goblet.

"This is feeling and warmth." He kissed her on the forehead. "We'll start ourselves and invite Kira and Maldir later, if we want to. Let's drink to friends, lovers, sharing, leaving. That's what's in my thoughts now, all intermingled.''

"You left your glass behind," Kerry said softly.

"We'll both drink from yours.''

He held the glass to her lips, then to his, taking no wine taster's sip but a generous mouthful. It was a big, hearty wine and could take it.

He took her down, not to the couch but to the floor. She helped eagerly with the clothes.

"Damon," she murmured. "Oh, Damon! Kira, too.'' She opened her body to him, her mind to Kira. "Yes, Maldir!''

It intermingled, it flooded. Images, rolls of passion and feeling, overlays. Kira, lupine and feminine, tongue lolling. Standing wide-legged, her head turned over her shoulder. Maldir approaching, stiff-legged and expectant, his penis red and engorged; dripping moisture as he circled to touch noses and lick Kira's snout, then nuzzle her swollen vulva. Other images, projected so that Kerry could sense them, not left suspended to be apprehended as the more subtle union of the Kindred might desire: Maldir as a red-bearded, work-muscled homesteader, coming to his cabin, body glistening with sweat. A woman, eager and open, awaiting him, leading him to a bed of cushions, cold drinks beside. Their union melded with this. Kira, a fair young girl in a summer dress, cool breezes of evening ruffling the down on her bare arms, reaching the skin beneath the dress as did a blond youth at her side. They coupled in a pleasure garden's wooded bower, beneath paper lanterns floating in the summer wind—easily and lightly as befitted a midsummer evening, a midsummer of decades past.

Kerry had raised herself to all fours and was turning her rear to Damon, her legs open, her inner lips swollen. Damon took her in long, slow strokes, letting her feel the slap of his belly, the swing of his balls against her upturned butt. He sensed her frenzy, counterpointed by an interior languor. He felt the steaminess of an African evening, the moon a hanging jewel in an ebon sky. Blackness all embracing: obsidian, volcanic. Spearheads, flint-hard and black. This had to be Kerry's image, remembrance. An Ethiop tribesman—strong, sensitive, powerful, hard.

The alienness, each to the others. The closeness, enveloping the four of them and those past lovers, reflected in a hall of mirrors that trailed off into the night. Nothing was articulated, nor had to be.

Disengagement.

Damon rose slowly to return with the decanter and his glass. Kerry leaned back against the bulk of the couch.

"Is it always this good?"

"No. It can be just a bacchanal. It depends on the participants."

"Did I help make it good for you and Kira and Maldir?"

"Very good. We have less to offer, in a way. No past existences, personas, to draw on. But we have an engaging alienness, I'm told. But this went beyond novelty. Even with the second and third born—maybe especially, particularly with the jaded ones—you get sensations, not feeling. I'll take feeling."

"Can we do it again?"

"Everyone would like that."

The lovemaking was slower, the overlays more subtle and varied—some only peripherally connected with lovemaking. Walks on black sand beaches. The ache in lungs and legs at the end of a testing foot race. The oiled stride of a lope through the forest. The pains and passions of childbirth. The exultation of discovery on a desert archeological dig. The holding close in complete darkness to a loved one, recognizable by touch, taste, and smell.

And something more.

Kira's pealing laughter, underlaid by a touch of contempt.

What is it?

Listen.

Go away, Malcolm, you old voyeur. This is a foursome.

Flush. Hotness. Flustered pulling away.

Don't feel put out, Kerry. This from Kira. *We*

*were projecting, not just opening. It must have reached
and attracted Gant.*

But he did hang around. Maldir was notably
amused.

*Consider it an amusement, Kerry. Not an intru-
sion. A little voyeurism has its savor.*

Kerry tried to keep the distaste from her thought:
Not when it's Gant!

Part III

TRANSIT ————————————

Damon pulled on the uniform shirt—stripped of all insignia of service and rank, but government issue summer tans just the same. A different feel: once familiar, now strange. Crisp and smooth to the skin, quite apart from the more free-form folds of the garments he had worn for eleven years. Aside from feel there was smell, the faint detergent-and-starch aroma of a shipboard laundry.

He took time to savor these highly novel impressions of a commonplace experience. It was somewhat like coming across and putting on a discarded snakeskin.

Not quite the same snakeskin. The absence of insignia attested to that. The closest parallel to his status was that of a tech rep, those representatives of the engineering companies sometimes on board to advise on the highly technical aspects of their firms' equipment and weaponry. Possessing officer's privileges but nowhere appearing in the chain of command, they were a phenomenon familiar to surface and space navies for centuries. Better, the Captain and Damon had agreed, to fit oneself into a preformed niche than to carve out a new one.

Damon walked slowly from his stateroom, provoking no unusual interest from enlisted men or officers as he made his way through the ship. Quite different from his first visit. His surface appearance no longer shouted of alienness.

Alienation, though—that was something else.

He'd have to overcome that. You can't stand aloof and hope to be a bridge, a conduit, an awakener. An idol, yes. A messiah. Even a prophet. These last were unwelcome roles. He would have to be accessible, could not live in alienation if he hoped to set humanity on a new path.

These were lofty, broad-gauged purposes. Damon had a set of very near-term aims: to get home without making waves and to get home alive.

In some form or other.

The ship was large, and Damon's passage through it could readily be regarded as a reorientation on this first day since lift-off. Of the same class as the *Fairbairn,* this ship held only minor refitting differences. Damon paused now and then to pay more attention than he really felt to redesigned hatch fittings and streamlined communications outlets. The basic locations of different compartments remained the same. He passed enlisted men and officers both, receiving no salutes or anyone of seniority looking for such. Each greeted Damon with a nod, which he returned equably. Apparently he had been the subject of a thorough briefing.

The ship's library made a pleasant way station in his wanderings, and Damon spent an hour bringing himself more current on Terran events. By the time this ship returned, well over twenty years would have elapsed since his last Earthside experiences. Only ten of them would have been in the library's archives. As Khan had predicted and Kerry had confirmed, the expansionist bloc had climbed to dominance. In the last couple of years of the chronicle, Damon could detect a loosening of the alliance. The eastern states were seemingly becoming disaffected, perhaps recognizing that colonization could never siphon off a major chunk of their population, only the aggressive and ambitious of them. Once that had been enough. Things were changing in the eastern lands. Damon wondered how much could be attributed to Khan's influence and those he advised.

Of the *Fairbairn* mission there was little mention. The discovery of another human or humanlike civilization must have been major news, but it had been subtly and capably played down. The picture rendered was one of a race in decline, possessing interesting vestiges of power and knowledge no longer used, perhaps incapable of being tapped by the descendants of that complex race who had opted for a life of simplicity. Or who had had it forced on them. A team of scientists would be dispatched, nonetheless, to see what could be salvaged from the remains. End of story.

Damon checked out a novel written since his time on Earth, by an author he had liked. One of the advantages of time dilation. The yeoman in charge of the library looked at him with appraising and inquisitive eyes. Damon gathered that he had plenty of time to survey the library's infrequent visitors. No matter that the holo theatres and arcades were always full.

"I hear that you have some additions for our library, sir. Mr. Chaudhuri brought some books and tapes in earlier today."

"Have you tried any?"

"Yes, sir. I'm working through the poetry of Danvers Kam."

"A good start." Damon nodded approvingly. "We're trying to bring back the best of hundreds of thousands of years of literature, music, art, from a great race. More than one race, actually. The Lydians have recorded and catalogued the works of other peoples, some of them long gone. Better put aside a lot of time for reading and listening."

"I always have, sir. But I think I'd need more than one lifetime."

Damon looked at the yeoman. Sensitive features, open eyes. He probed very lightly, reaching only for feel and awareness. An active and open mind. His children might have that option of more than one lifetime. Perhaps the yeoman himself. Damon left, promising to return often—for the yeoman's sake as well as Damon's own, though he left that aspect unspoken.

Damon's eventual objective was the wardroom for lunch. He doubted that he would get there. Walking slowly, he started in that direction again in meandering, exploratory fashion via the after portion of the ship. There, among various engineering compartments, was Secondary Conn.

The bridge and Combat Information Center held the only other two accesses to the programming circuits of the ship's main computer. In constant occupancy by large watch teams, both of these were out of the question. But here, deep in the after portion of the ship, was Secondary Conn, where the ship could be controlled and fought if the bridge and CIC were disabled. It was normally manned only by a quartermaster and a very junior officer—but a qualified Officer of the Deck nonetheless—and it made for the most boring of watches.

Damon stood in the passageway, the hatch access panel before him, and took a deep and calming breath.

The handle was cold and metallic, solid to the grip. He turned the dogleg and swung open the hatch.

The room was darkened, the watch officer and quartermaster watching a holo in the quiet and black interior. Quite permissible on this standby-type watch where nothing happened, and alarms would galvanize attention if anything did.

The lieutenant switched off the holo and activated the red light, enabling him to see in the semidarkness. He quickly recognized Damon.

"Can't allow you to visit, Mr. Hart. You're not authorized personnel."

Damon had hoped for some temporizing small talk but wasn't going to find it.

He went in along the neural raceways, quickly freezing the motor functions of the lieutenant and his quartermaster. They stared at him from their seats through unblinking eyes. The lieutenant's blue eyes looked at Damon in immobile fear and puzzlement. Damon addressed himself to the fear, projecting to both men reassurance and a measure of calm. It took much of his consciousness to handle this kind of two-person control.

Past their line of vision and over to the access terminal. There was a double security system here— the limited physical access of bridge, CIC and Secondary Conn, and password control. Damon extracted the password from the lieutenant's mind and entered it into the computer.

The screen acknowledged access and Damon punched in: MASTER PROGRAM. COMMANDS FOLLOW:

OPEN P TERMINAL.

Damon felt the psi receptivity of the terminal unshielding.

IMPRINT FOR AUTHORIZED ACCESS. ACKNOWLEDGE WHEN IMPRINTING COMPLETE.

Damon waited, projecting what he could to the terminal. A tough proposition, complicated by the control he was having to exert. He took a chance and released control over the watch officer and quarter-master.

"Don't move. I'll reestablish control if you do."

A slight shifting of weight was the only response from the watch team. Damon concentrated on reaching the psi terminal, an unauthorized adjunct to the computer and one whose existence was beyond the knowledge of its designers or shipboard personnel.

IMPRINTING COMPLETE.

It felt good to ease off projecting. Too soon to relax. One step remained.

ERASE RECORD OF PRIOR INSTRUCTIONS. ACKNOWL-EDGE.

ADDITIONAL COMMAND CODE REQUIRED.

Damon had that from Cortald Dir, who had arranged the circuitry to establish the psi terminal during the outbound passage. Damon entered the code.

ERASURE COMPLETED.

Damon took the computer out of programming and

back to normal mode. He turned to the quartermaster and the watch officer. They were still in their seats and facing slantwise across the room.

"As you were," Damon said, using the ritual at-ease expression of a superior officer. "I won't go in again and I'm sorry I had to at all. Consider it an unfortunate necessity from my point of view."

The young officer was standing now, holding on to a stanchion for support. His blond hair clung damply to his forehead. His voice was shaky but showed feistiness.

"I'm going to have to report this to the bridge. Now, if you'll let me, but later anyway."

"Quite right of you. But they know already."

A shrill bosun's pipe whistled through the compartment's annunciator, followed by words of imperative command. "Mr. Hart, lay up to the bridge! Mr. Hart, to the bridge!" A slight pause. "On the double!"

Damon rose from the terminal panel.

"I'm off to the bridge. Go ahead and make your report."

This time he took the direct route. He knew it well. No nods from those he met en route. Enlisted men, officers, even up to commander rank, all stood aside as Damon strode toward the summons.

Too bad it had to come to this. There was no way to block the computer from displaying at the bridge that it was being programmed—short of being in the computer to block it. Paradoxically, it was that access that he was setting up.

Damon would have preferred this upcoming confrontation later. No real choice, though. It had been immediately imperative that he insure being alive to meet it, whenever.

The bridge was in ferment, the watch team of OOD, JOOD, helmsman, messengers, and quartermasters intent on his arrival. The Captain, sitting on the edge of his captain's chair, sprang out of it to assert command at once.

"Mr. Hart—kindly accompany me to my cabin. You too, Dr. Gant."

The cabin was no less cramped than Damon remembered it. The Captain moved to his chair and sat down. Damon and Gant stood, neither being offered the sole chair remaining, and neither likely to.

The Captain went at it with no preamble and some display of controlled anger. "Prior to your actions, Dr. Gant was trying to convince me, Mr. Hart, to have you confined to quarters for the duration of the passage home. He seems to think you dangerous. I considered his suggestion unwarranted and implicitly contrary to our earlier agreement, but I'll say now that you're proving his point. What do you have to say in justification of your behavior?"

Damon met the Captain's eyes directly.

"I don't doubt that Dr. Gant—or should I say Commander Gant?—considers me dangerous, though more to his ambitions than to this ship or Earth itself.'' Damon paused. ''I acted, Captain, through concern for my safety. It may be only you who can confine me to quarters, but Dr. Gant can do far worse.''

''What do you mean?''

''He can kill me. Or have me killed.''

The Captain tightened his lips in what Damon hoped was genuine dismissal and disbelief. ''Are you seriously suggesting such a thing? Aside from the implausibility of such an accusation from out of no-where, I understand that you possess considerable psi powers.''

Damon looked over at Gant, whose face was imperturbable.

''So does Dr. Gant. And it doesn't take special powers to do in even a psi adept. There are any number of mechanical booby traps that can be preset, even those that will trigger on a psi probe. Or there's poison. Or anything similar. So long as there are confines to a person's body—even the dimensions of this ship—anyone is vulnerable.'' Damon turned back to face the Captain head-on. ''Tell me, Captain, are you aware of the circumstances of the death of the *Fairbairn*'s captain?''

''His gig blew up.'' The Captain drew in his lower lip pensively. ''Yes, I see your point. There were the motions of an investigation, but nothing could be proved.'' He slammed his fist down on his desk and shifted his gaze angrily between Damon and Gant. "Damn it! I will *not* have such maneuverings on this ship!"

"And yet, if Dr. Gant were to kill or immobilize me—no matter how farfetched a possibility—you couldn't resurrect me, nor even do much to punish Dr. Gant. At most, you could restrain him, confine him to quarters. Am I correct?"

"It's true that Dr.—Commander—Gant has recently shown me credentials which have been authenticated by the mission instructions entered in the computer. He has broad plenipotentiary powers—in fact, is to be Earth's lead negotiator with all alien races encountered on this trip. Indeed, he can alter and select planetfalls to this end. And yes, I am particularly constrained from interfering in his relations with you." The Captain's face showed visible distaste.

"That, also, is contrary to our prior agreement," Damon said. "But I understand that you can't be bound beyond your constituted authority. I had that limitation once."

"You still do," Gant said.

"Mac, that's your opinion." Damon turned again to the Captain. "That's why I had to act."

"Will you tell me what you entered into the computer?"

Damon thought a moment. The Captain had turned around somewhat and was buying Damon's version, at least in part. Possibly distaste for Gant and his capacity for subverting the Captain's power and even changing the direction of his mission had something to do with that. The Captain was inviting the response Damon wanted to give by making a request, not issuing an order whose flouting could escalate the confrontation.

"I can't, I'm afraid. But I will tell you that it bore on improving my survival chances and restraining Dr. Gant. There'll be no need of my infringing on any off-limits areas again—so long as I'm not life threatened."

The Captain pushed back from his desk, his arms stiff against it. His eyes swept from Damon to Gant and to Damon again.

"I'm going to take you at your word, Mr. Hart. Be warned that any further such excursion will merit confinement." He held up a hand to Gant, who was starting to mouth his protest. "No, Dr. Gant—*I* shall make these decisions on my ship. Its safety is still *my* paramount concern and responsibility, no matter what yours is. I see nothing in my orders or your credentials that contravenes that. And I order you explicitly—I never thought I'd have to issue such an order on a ship of mine—to commit no action that provokes a fight that would endanger this ship. No matter what your position and power at home, you shall obey that command."

Gant moved his lips, but thought better of speaking aloud.

"Now, you two are dismissed!"

Gant left first. Damon turned at the hatch and gave a brief nod to the Captain, who had sat down again at his desk. He stared out and beyond and did not acknowledge.

Damon secured the hatch behind him, then turned to Kerry. She had her blouse unbuttoned already, making no effort to restrain her hunger. Not waiting for his willing help, she pulled the blouse from her waistband and dropped it to the floor. The nipples of her small breasts were hard and upturned, though the room was warm.

She gave Damon and the room an appraising glance. With a toss of her head she loped forward and bounced off her rear leg, driving her right arm through her legs and tucking. She came up to her feet, arms at the ready. A good judo roll up.

"Nice room. Good for any number of sports." She walked slowly toward him, her face flushed. "It's larger than my torture chamber of a stateroom. Or did you choose it because you've got a jock fetish?"

There was an air to the place, all right. An odor of *tatami* still clung faintly to the mats, long exiled from their native Japan. An authentic and valued anachronism. It dominated the more recent residues of perspiration, cutting the sourness and blending it with the aroma of real straw. There were chalk and resin to dust the air from their boxes near the bars and vaulting horse. The rings hung from the ceiling on ropes of real hemp. There was something to this room beyond the metal and plastic of a fighting ship. Even the sweat was that of exuberant exertion, not the combat stink of apprehension and fear.

Their sex did have an element of exuberance and acrobatics, lacking since lift-off. It was a release, a celebration. Fun. A cutting loose from shipboard routine and the need for vigilance.

Kerry and the room brought it all home. Kerry lay beside him, warm and yielding now, hot and demanding before. The image and remembrance of Kira overlaid him now and always, a vibrancy of light at his very core. He felt Kerry move as she picked up on this. She was too much to him now for him to hide it.

"Kerry. Kira. The loves of my life. Can I say it?"

"Can you not?" She moved her lips slowly down his belly, then sideways to his hip and the edge of his butt. She nipped it.

Damon sat up sharply to meet her laughter and her projection of a wolfish muzzle harrying his flanks.

Kira, Kerry. Mischief never far beneath the hunger. Kira was now a receding presence, one of the images in the hall of mirrors that would reflect on all his emotional encounters. She was gone to him in any other guise, perhaps forever. Kerry was emerging, ripening into Kira's depth and meaning for Damon. He was evolving too. He could see the direction, not the end.

Damon lay back on the cool mat, eyes on the featureless ceiling. Kerry had squirmed sideways, resting her head on his belly, his hands in her thick, coppery hair.

"We'll do it again here," she said softly. "Though we *could* try my stateroom. What's your objection?"

"It's pretty certainly bugged. Not that I mind a little exhibitionism now and again. But not with Gant on the other end. Enough's enough."

"Son of a bitch!" She sat up sharply. "He wouldn't!"

"Sure he would. And not openly and lasciviously in that dirty middle-aged man role you've cast him in. More in his savior-of-humanity pose. From me, of course. Or his personal power trip. Don't underestimate the lengths he'd go to."

"Stoop to!"

"Worse than you think. I'll bet that my stateroom is booby-trapped so that I can be immobilized or killed in some preset, mechanical way. Probably several compartments. This ship was outfitted to be a death chamber. They didn't know back home what they'd be getting in me, and they'd be right in character in planning my control or removal. Prudent by their reckoning."

"Murderous by mine. Why don't you move out?"

"That's no protection. In a closed environment anyone's pretty easy to kill, particularly if you don't care about covering your tracks."

Kerry shivered and reached for her blouse. "Gant. You know, I used to come to this room for workouts on the trip out. Gant was always looking for judo partners, mainly me. I think he'd rather take me down in a missed throw than drop me cleanly. He'd like to roll around with me on the *tatami*."

"He cheats," Damon said. Kerry raised an eyebrow. "He's a good *judoka* but not as good as his results. He anticipates well. Perhaps too well." Damon paused. "Giving him the benefit, maybe in the heat of competition he's not aware that he's reading."

"He'd better not let the others know," Kerry said. "He'll never get workout partners."

"I've got a tough one for you." Damon reached for Kerry's hand. "Don't provoke him openly. I mean it partly for your own safety. Don't make it a Burns/Hart alliance versus Gant."

"Well, he's still after me sexually. Maybe our thing titillates him further. Or maybe he wants to pump me in all sorts of ways. About you—on a purely professional basis, of course." Damon laughed and so did she. "Actually, I do respect him professionally, and our fields do overlap. He won't believe that my professional regard doesn't carry over to his person."

"Keep the lines open," Damon said. "At least till we get through this next landfall. I'm not allowed any overt contact with this planet's natives, but you can learn and play the watchdog."

"Alien Contact's in an uproar." Kerry looked up from buttoning her blouse. "Commander De Silva's not taking too kindly to being preempted and having Gant lead the contact team."

"I don't doubt it. But Gant's picked this system and his credentials and his clout let him. Trouble is, he's working off data tens of thousands of years old, from before the Lydians reached their current development. We're going to be meeting the descendants of their malcontents of tens of millennia ago, when they thought in terms of colonization as a solution to handling misfits. They hadn't developed their psi powers to their current state, but who knows where they are now? Perhaps that's the appeal to Gant. I suppose he thinks he can manipulate them or at least learn more from them than he got elsewhere."

"Can he?"

"Again, who knows? The city archives have nothing current on that ancient and remote colony. And I think he's taking the planet's indigenous natives far too lightly. Thinks his psi shielding can protect him, come what may."

"Nomadic grazers," Kerry said. "As I recall it, horses or horselike. No technology, no manipulative appendages. But with some psi powers."

"Perhaps more than Mac Gant bargains for," Damon said. "His type has to be shown, not told."

"Roger thinks the ship is haunted," Kerry said. She sat deep in her armchair, looking out at the wardroom and its amusements with an anthropologist's eye, her legs tucked under her.

Damon looked up from his book. He had long outgrown the desire to participate in wardroom revelries; even spectating palled. Where Kerry could watch in amused cynicism, his cynicism was more sour and better not aroused. "Does he find that disturbing?" he asked, swinging his attention to the absent Chabron. "I'd find the idea intriguing, but then, I'm not Roger."

"I'd hope not. No, Roger has detected traces of an unseen presence aboard and, yes, it does disturb him. It manifests itself mainly in the computer, of course, or he'd never know. Prometheus could parade on the forecastle and Roger would light his pipe from his torch without taking notice."

Damon closed his book and put it aside. "What sort of 'unseen presence'? Sounds quite unlike Roger to me. If he's ever had a metaphysical speculation—much less one bordering on the occult—I've never heard it. Too unscientific."

"Roger describes it in several terms, some scientific. He doesn't really understand it, and he's pussy-footing around it. An anomaly, he says. A few moments later he calls it a ghost in the computer. I asked him whether the latter was some current computer buzz word, if he was viewing the phenomenon with scientific eyes—or did he intend the common meaning of 'ghost' and was looking at it with country superstition.''

Damon laughed. ''Not too sympathetic a response. Poor Roger. You don't treat him well.''

Kerry looked at him appraisingly. ''I'm *not* sympathetic *with* Roger, though he'd like to think himself Gallicly sympathetic *to* me. He's made that plenty clear many times over a couple of years. It's you I lust for, and don't forget it!''

''I don't, and I don't want to.'' Damon paused. ''I'm surprised he hasn't tried this one on his demigod, Gant. The logical choice, and Roger's logical, if nothing else.''

''Roger's scared of Gant. Question is, is he more scared of what he can't see, can't track down and explain—and in his own bailiwick? That's a tough one for someone like Roger to take.''

''He could ask me,'' Damon said.

''He's scared of you, too. There's a paradox here. He's not afraid of approaching anyone who can't help him—like me—but he can't bring himself to go to the Captain or you. My guess is that he'll eventually try Gant, and that they'll try to beard you together. Gant's not the man to let this lie.''

''Not my idea of a fun evening.'' Damon shook

his head. "But I'll make myself accessible nonetheless. Anything to put a damper on Roger's fears and Mac's ambitions. Not to mention paranoia. I sure hope they don't set it up as a confrontation, though. I've had more than enough of that."

Mac Gant had been conducting himself somewhat ominously of late, making Chabron's fears understandable. Gant was often alone in his quarters— collating his data, he said—or in sick bay. His presence and his higher rank had quite overpowered the ship's medical officer. A mild man, he had been left to tend to the real and imagined ailments of a bored crew while Gant took over the laboratory facilities and much of sick bay's administrative apparatus as his duchy. The medical corpsmen, eager for any stimulation, had become his assistants in this "collation of data." His praetorian guard also, it was rumored.

No wonder Chabron was intimidated. Gant's current self-elevation was bad enough. And Chabron certainly couldn't relish past memories—his service as handmaiden to Gant's attempt at breaking into the Lydian computer and its internal worlds. Plus the ultimate embarrassing denouement—and who better than a Frenchman to suffer and understand it: to be discovered as helpless, then—in front of a computer!

Still, puzzlement and fear did it. It must have. Within a couple of days of Kerry's having voiced Chabron's revelations and misgivings, he and Gant

approached Damon as he sat in his accustomed armchair in the same corner of the wardroom. Damon
knew that he was making himself predictable. That
had its plus and minus sides. As a junior officer on
the *Fairbairn*'s trip out, Damon hadn't had a power
base or even an office—until Commander Harding's
death had catapulted him to department head of Alien
Contact. On this return trip he was a figure of vague
and undefinable status. Practically no status, *ex offi-
cio*. It had come full circle. Aside from a cramped
stateroom, a quiet corner of the wardroom was
Damon's retreat, his office, his den—as it had been
when he had played chess with Rachman Khan and
had been initiated into the higher realms of shipboard
and Earthside bareknuckled politics.

Gant was no Rachman Khan. His approach did not
evince pleasurable anticipation in Damon. Gant's purpose was surely not to illuminate, rather to probe.
The neurophysiologist stood assertively before Damon,
blocking Damon's field of vision should he look up.
Damon didn't, though not all that immersed in his
book of the moment, till Gant resorted to the sounds
and motion of an impatient foot shuffling. Damon
put his book aside and regarded Gant with an air of
puzzled inquiry, quite soundless. Behind Gant,
Chabron went through his own brand of nervous
shuffling.

"Could we have a word with you, Damon?" Gant
asked, composedly enough.

"Of course, Mac." Damon tapped the adjoining chair and waved to another across the room. "Roger, pull one up from over there."

"I thought sick bay might be a better choice," Gant replied. Damon raised an eyebrow. "More privacy there," Gant went on. "And more importantly, there's a terminal in sick bay with rather liberal access coding. Roger and I would like to enlist your aid in researching some anomalies he's turned up in the computer."

Damon stood up and stretched out a kink in his shoulder. "Sounds more like Roger's field, but let's have a look. You'd better lead the way, Mac. I've been too well to remember the way to sick bay."

"Try to stay that way. It's better."

Damon looked at Gant sharply. If there was a double meaning here, Gant was not intent on belaboring it. "I've been working out at the gym," Gant went on. Apparently this was his idea of small talk to fill the time as they strode through the ship's passageways. "Best way to stay fit and out of sick bay. If you don't work there. I wish I could prescribe it for the ship's malingerers and make it stick. But they know their medical rights these days as well as their other ones."

Damon wondered when Gant had last seen a medical case or prescribed anything.

The on-duty medical corpsmen came to their feet

and saluted snappily as Gant led Damon and Roger into sick bay. Gant addressed the enlisted men by name as he gave them his "as you were" response. Damon took it in. There was an air of purposefulness to the place—yeomen typing on terminal keyboards, bustling in an uncommon way. It wasn't sick call hours or even normal duty hours, but the place was vibrantly alive.

Gant strode through sick bay as if he owned it. The stories seemed true. He likely did. Damon quickly found himself in the main laboratory and in front of a computer terminal. Gant shooed the laboratory personnel out, and they left unquestioningly, halting their work in midprocess, so it seemed. They, too, had been hard at it. But at what? Gant waited till they had all exited, the last securing the hatch behind him, then turned to Chabron. "Explain it, Roger. What you've found. Or not found."

"It's hard to explain," Chabron began hesitatingly. "The technical terms . . ."

"Can the technical terms, Roger. You explained it to me, and I'm a layman in cybernetics. Just sketch the outline. I rather think that Damon can tell us the rest. Or access it. If he wants to."

"There's *something* in there," Chabron said. He seemed perpetually nervous in Gant's presence. He couldn't keep his fingers still. They clenched and curled, moved randomly, not at all as an aid to verbal expression. "Maybe it's a program where there wasn't one before. A shadow program. I can tell there's something because it *influences* other programs in subtle ways. Some standard programs have even been modified to greater efficiency in ways I've never seen done by Terran programmers."

"But you've seen those telltales before," Damon prompted. Gant looked on attentively.

"Yes. On Lydia."

"Well, then. Maybe someone's done you and the ship's computer a good turn. But there's more to this, or so you think?"

"Yes. It's a shifting influence. Its manifestations are changing *now*. We're not talking past history, past doings. Something shifting and variable is in the computer and I can't trace or access it."

Damon sat back in his chair, gauging Chabron's consternation. Chabron reached over his shoulder to activate the terminal. Damon was brought aware of Chabron's odor as well. His shirt was soaked at the armpits.

"Let me," Damon said softly, and Chabron jumped. His hands pulled back from the keyboard as though it were hot.

Damon punched in the password so that both Gant and Chabron could see it displayed. CORTALD DIR.

"You there, Cortald?" Damon asked.

"Yes, Damon." The voice resonated in bass tones

from the dual speakers to their side. Chabron jumped again. Gant nodded his head and smiled.

"I have Mac Gant and Roger Chabron with me, Cortald. You'll know them from their voices. They've discovered you, and I'm sure they'd like to ask you some questions."

"Perhaps later," Gant said. "Would you excuse us, Cortald, while we deactivate this terminal? I'd rather ask Damon some questions before talking with you." Without waiting for a response, Gant reached over Damon's shoulder and powered off the terminal.

"Cortald Dir," Gant stated flatly. "He's the Lydian who traveled back to Earth with the *Fairbairn*, then back home with us. Out-of-body. All unbeknownst, until we arrived at Lydia."

"That's right."

"I should go to the Captain with this."

But you've learned not to risk confrontations you won't win, where you're less than fully informed, haven't you, Mac? Just your and Roger's suspicions wouldn't have done it. But now I've given your 'menace' a name and an identity. And I'm sure you view Cortald Dir as a threat—to your plans, at least. I've also given you access to Cortald. To use as a demonstration to the Captain and others. Or to summon for yourself to use. Or to influence, do you imagine? Okay, Mac—what now?

Damon kept these thoughts shielded. Little need.

Gant was too busy weighing the complicated permutations of the situation, and its implications, to probe.

Gant went on ruminatively, "But I think we have something more than a stowaway here. Or should I say less?"

"Very good, Mac," Damon said. "Keep going."

"If it *were* Cortald Dir, we couldn't very well shut him off with a switch. He could shut us off more readily. So what do we have here?" Gant looked at Damon directly. "Some sort of simulacrum?"

"Pretty much. It's a program of Cortald Dir, crafted *by* Cortald—his legacy to the ship. It's set up to answer as he would—with his values and cognitive abilities—to any query he could anticipate. And that covers a lot of ground. You can discuss philosophic and metaphysical questions with it—him. That was his main area of interest. You can learn from him, if you're willing. More pragmatically, you can ask him what he would do in a given situation. Such as: 'Ought we to contact this former colony of theirs, the expedition you've been pushing for?' Just load in enough data if he doesn't have it in his or the ship's banks already. But the whole construct is just a super program. Cortald Dir doesn't roam the ship incorporeally. You have to summon his simulacrum and *ask*."

Damon paused and looked at the laboratory instrumentation about him. "If you've got a scanner here to help place the electrodes, you can try wiring your-self up as you did on Lydia and go into the computer yourself. Meet Cortald more on his terms. He'd be more than just a disembodied voice then. You might like it."

Gant smiled ineffably and nodded his negative. Words were not needed.

"What *does* he say about approaching this world of Mac's?" Chabron asked querulously into the silence. Gant stared Chabron down, and the cyberneticist retreated a step. The air hummed on several real and other less tangible levels, the high voltage sounds of laboratory machines and power politics.

"He says not to," Damon said. "But you had that advice on Lydia."

"So we did," Gant said dismissively. He stood up, joining Chabron, whose nervous restlessness had never permitted him to take a seat throughout the encounter. "Thank you for your help, Damon," Gant added formally, dismissing the man as he had the argument. Or trying to.

"A moment, Mac," Chabron said with an unex-pected flash of temerity. "I have a few more points I'd like cleared up."

"Of a technical nature, I imagine," Gant said from the chair into which he settled in the man-ner of a seigneur. "Do so, Roger. Ask Damon. But not here, if you please. I have no more questions of

Damon. He's told me quite enough and given me plenty to chew on. I think I'd like to do that—alone.''

Damon slipped off his clothes, standing up. A common water tumbler on the desktop caught the rays of the stateroom's glow lamp and splintered and refracted them uncommonly. He folded his trousers carefully over the chair, tossed his shirt carelessly into a corner.

Going out-of-body could be an abrasive neural wrench. It could also be a frictionless slippage.

Damon lay on his bunk, in silence, now in the dark. He marshaled his essence, called wandering tendrils of thought in, drew in to a pinpoint, a nuclear core that had no mass. He held it, collapsed it, then let his being nova out, past the confines of brainpan and skull. Out-of-body.

The ship. Damon felt its pulse, its vibrancy, its solidity in nothingness. Its star-driven nothingness in the real space it had left. It was alive in its way and by the standards of some of the dimensions in which it traveled. There were thousands of minds aboard, each encased in its personal sphere. In leaving his own body, Damon felt no desire to reach out to other minds, to disturb their deeper slumber or the few that searched. Neither did he shun their nontouching proximity. And all contempt, even for the meanest spirit, washed away.

Beyond the ship. Warp and twist and bend. Light. Song. Incomprehensibility.

Time. Timelessness. Time as a precondition to eternity.

And eventually back, not yet to his body or to anyone else's. Not even to the two minds—Kerry's and Vijay's—he could cherish and value. Through the ship to the psi terminal where Cortald Dir slept and waited and could talk around such questions as could never be answered.

Part IV

GRASSLANDS KING

Men have given me many names. I have come to value them as I value those who name me.

Grasslands King. King of Plain and Waste. Death Dealer. They all contain truth along with the hyperbole—even this last. And I abhor that name most of all. I have killed my own kind when they ask it as a mercy, but I had not yet killed any man for that reason (and some had asked), nor for defense or retribution. Yet I have been trained to do so and knew I would one day if I lived long enough. The odds were with it.

Men seldom venture into our domain of grassland plains. They stick to their towns. Denied motor vehicles, they lack the will and the need to maintain their roads. Their highways are cracked and uptilted through water seepage, and inexorable pressure of plant growth through their gaps, earth upheavals. Their cities are dead. The size of their towns is limited by the capacity of the outlying farmlands. And there are some who live in isolation.

To such we are indeed dealers of death, if but indirectly. The father whose child lies dying with a burst appendix can well shake his fist at those who deny him transport. Five thousand years ago a man could rail against fate, but men today know of cars, airplanes, and laser scalpels, even if they have never seen them. And they know wherein lies that denial.

Men may not care to come to us, nor we to them, but yet we must. For self-preservation we must monitor attempts at technology and discourage them—by death in the last resort, and that is how we earn our name. Despite man's inward philosophic focus of the last few thousand years, there are some not of this bent: those who are born to speculate technologically and to tinker. Most of mankind fears the consequences. They remember the Grasslands Wars, whose casualties reduce a child with a burst appendix to a minor statistic. These are our allies and, occasionally, our informants. Our spies, to draw a less fine line. But others rebel, support the drive to technological rediscovery.

We can sympathize but can ill afford to indulge these tendencies.

It was ill luck that I was gone when the disturbance came to light. The herd in the great canyon across the ford had a mare queen of my generation. I had been sent from my home herd to rule my present one with this in mind. She carried the psi genes as did I. A mating would increase the probability of a foal with the gift, and I was making my first visit since leaving the psi herd and taking my place as head of my group on the western grasslands.

There is no reason why a planned mating should not carry the pleasure and eroticism of a spontaneous rut. Haneel knew this. She kept up an impish attitude of mock indecision, though her hormones were rapidly driving her to animalistic desire even if her spirit should find mine unattractive. It evidently did not, as she let me know, but still—

We're young, my friend—it is so burdensome to carry a foal in the summer heat. Shall I suppress the hormones and we can wait till fall? We can run off our energies on the Outback Plains and try again next season.

I looked into her eyes, too inexperienced to tell the gleam of mischief from that of the tease. I nudged her muzzle with mine and slid around, brushing my shoulder along her legs and flank, ducking down to nuzzle and lick her loins. The sharp odors and taste were intoxicating.

With a shudder she skittered aside, so that I could once more meet her eyes. I began to learn that the gleam in them could be both mischief and erotic anticipation.

She galloped off, letting me chase behind. She made sure to go not so far nor so fast as to burn off all our energies. I caught her—or she me—in a stream-fed box canyon, and learned how agreeably duty could mix with pleasure.

When we returned, a messenger from my herd awaited. Haneel's folk were in agitation. Dust flew where more ground had been pawed than at the Solstice Games. We are an open people, and Marda had communicated to all the import as well as the urgency of the situation. It was simple enough.

One of our outrangers had been killed by men near the town of Blye. His companion had seen it from a distance, heard the mindscream. Lacking greater psi powers, he could only flee and bring the word.

No man had killed one of my herd for generations. Nor we one of them. And this had been no deranged-individual act. It had been a group action, done after hospitality had been extended and accepted. The ranger had sensed the unrest but lacked the capacity to probe deeper than surface thought. They would not have gotten me so easily. But they would soon have the chance to try in some more devious way.

There were some of Haneel's advisers who urged me not to go. Haneel, almost, but she knew our duty. She lent me one of her number as a messenger and flanker. She let me know, also, how fine our mating had been and how she longed to carry our foal. No coquetry now. I was moved as I once again looked into her eyes and beyond, to the eye of her mind.

I wheeled and followed my companions.

The path along the river was shaded and cool with forage aplenty. But we were not hungry. The river itself had pools and shallow runs where I had disported on my trip to meet Haneel. When we plunged into the spray or pools it was now for needed refreshment only.

Then we reached the ford and splashed across to our home prairie, moving away from the river's coolness and striking out cross-country. There was no well-traveled route to follow, but the way was clear. Often we passed rusted posts and wire, and farmhouses abandoned centuries ago. A few had wells with levers that both we and men could manipulate to bring water bubbling into the trough. Men had been more hospitable then—until we let them know that no amount of water access could make up for the reduction of our grasslands by their farms. The forage was good here. Wheat and rye gone to seed, intermingled with wild oats and native grasses. We were hungrier now.

We pressed on, crossing buckled roads obliquely and not using them for our passage till we neared Blye and its outlying farms. Here was fencing in more modern repair—wood fencing, to be sure, but fencing nonetheless. We would be forced to use the road. I sent Marda ahead. She went unflinchingly. I sent my probes farther ahead, around, behind as well. Haneel's lieutenant took position well to the rear. My range was good, and I was able to station him at crossings of the main road, so that he could strike off into the fields and the plains beyond. I leapfrogged him from crossroad to crossroad as Marda and I advanced toward the town. Fields and farmhouses gave way to storeblocks and plazas, and the impressions of human minds, familiar and newly oppressive, impinged in greater depth. I could feel them behind storefronts, behind the curtains of the lodgings above the stores, in their halls and taverns, their schools and offices. I saw no men on the streets nor children at play. It was early morning yet, not hot enough to drive men into the taverns, the stuccoed interiors, the ferned and lush courtyards that they favored at noontime. Yet no one was in sight.

I sensed their minds, though, and I did more. I projected the aura of who I was: Grasslands King. King of Plain and Waste. And for the first time ever, I with purpose overlaid my aura with the tinge of Death Dealer.

Was it that which emptied the road before us? We issued out and across the large square that was Blye's produce market. The stalls were empty of people, but there was a wild profusion of color. Fruits and vegetables spilled their ripeness to the eye, but only our eyes observed. No hand pinched, no hand weighed, no hand stole. The Blye shopkeepers and their patrons were gone.

We picked our way across the market square to the council hall and the horse sanctuary nearby. The silence was uncharacteristic and chilling. In its emptiness our unshod hooves rang on the stones louder than once steel-shod had done.

Marda disappeared from sight as she neared the sanctuary, the road falling away beneath her hooves in a rumble of dirt and cobbles. With mind and ear I heard her shriek as stakes impaled her gut. I probed her mind and dealt her swiftly the death that would come more cruelly and at greater length were I not there. I wheeled my mind around and probed, probed, probed till I found the Prime Councilor and summoned him forth to the pit where Marda lay, within ten paces of our people's shrine. I warned my remaining companion to renewed vigilance and locked a portion of my energies to a mind conduit with his. It was a drain and reduced my other capabilities, but it was a necessity nonetheless.

The great double doors of the council hall opened, each swung wide by a halberdier in formal livery. The Councilor came forth. Around his neck hung the great chain of office. None followed; he strode forth alone with steady pace, his mind unwavering as well. He bore his office well. I'll give him that.

I let him and those within know the depth of my

anger and my control of it. As he stopped before me, eyeing me and not the pit where Marda lay, I let my mind speak to him alone.

Shall I destroy the town or simply you and your council?

Better those responsible for this, of whom I am one. It was agreed that those who forced the play would pay the wager.

I considered the point.

Agreed. But the price of my forebearance is knowledge. Why?

I might have forced the knowledge from him, but I feared concentrating my powers to that task while still maintaining the mind link to my companion. There would be precious little left for a vigilance guard. But the Councilor answered freely.

A ship from outside has landed beyond the town on the other side. Its crew are men, or nearly so, though not of our home world. Some of us hope to enlist their technology to raise ours and to break the Compact. The more time we have, the better. The traps we laid were to buy time.

The sun was riding higher now, its orange rays slanting over the plaza, glancing off the glazed tiles of the sanctuary roof beyond the Councilor's shoulder.

There was something more here, and I needed to know it.

Why can I not persuade these men to leave this world, or slay them if they will not?

The Councilor smiled. *They speak only. They cannot make the mind link. One has some sensitivities but still falls short. Another has a psi shield, rudimentary but interesting. We would learn more of it, as you can imagine. As for the rest—we can read them in a fuzzy, conceptual way. They cannot read us at all.*

I understood. *You think I cannot reach them, then. I can, of course, find one or more of you to speak for me, if this be true. Willingly if possible, or I can force it.*

But can you slay them? he asked.

I paused.

Any of them, he continued. *But particularly the one with the psi shield.*

The Councilor had spoken of wagers. It was a high-stakes game indeed.

I can destroy this whole town, save one or two, and force communication on our terms. Keep it a local affair.

We have sent messengers to other towns. They will send messengers to towns beyond. Soon the whole world of men will know the news.

I bade my surviving companion depart at once to bear this intelligence to the psi herd. I enjoined him to vigilance and held my silence till he outdistanced my range, running free on the plains beyond. Then I turned to the Councilor, who waited expectantly. I slew him, then, and summoned his deputy forth. A lesser man in every way, he came with more of a faltering mien than his superior, and his knees buckled as he eyed the Councilor's corpse. I had not allowed him a death of dignity.

The deputy Councilor flinched at my gaze as the Councilor had not.

Take me to the ship.

"They're not telling us everything," Kerry said, looking at Gant and Commander De Silva. "But what else do we want to know? Do we stay here and keep hammering away, wrap it up and go home, or start over elsewhere?"

"None of the towns are larger than this," Gant replied. He looked at Kerry with an imperiousness of command that she found more disagreeable than imposing. "In fact, they're all about the same. And this group has learned our language already."

"Took them all of two days to do it," Kerry shot back. "Hardly surprising. According to the Lydian archives—and you've clearly delved into this obscure bit of esoterica far deeper than I have—the people here are the remnants of their own exploratory missions of—what?—a hundred thousand years ago? Dissatisfied malcontents, if I read it rightly. So what do you expect to get from them?"

Gant smiled ineffably and said nothing.

"I'd agree," Commander De Silva said dryly. He might have been preempted by Gant, but he intended to get his views on record. "They're less than open with us. And they keep stalling on getting us together with these horse creatures, or whatever they are. The ones they have their Great Compact with. The indigenous natives. That's who we should be dealing with."

"I wonder." Gant looked about him coolly, clearly unwilling to volunteer much. Kerry felt herself on the edge of exasperation.

"Come on, Mac," Kerry said. "What are you after here? Surely you're not trying that colonization number again. And if you are, it's not the men of this world we should be dealing with. The horse folk are its original inheritors."

Kerry looked at Gant and found disagreement in his bearing and his answer. "Has it occurred to you two that these people might be more open with their psi talents than the Lydians? On that world I had to wring out every bit of data myself. They gave me damned little help. These people might be willing to trade psi instruction and some practical education for the technology they've lost. Or been forced to give up. That would be worth a permanent mission here. Call it that if you don't like the word *colony*."

"The Lydians saw you as a less than suitable candidate for instruction," Kerry pointed out.

"Interesting. You seem privy to all sorts of information. From Hart, no doubt. In any case, even should we want to contact these horse creatures— and I'm not sure we do—we'd need these people and their telepathic powers to reach them. They run free on the plains and seldom visit the towns."

"I wouldn't worry about it overly," Commander De Silva said acerbically. He stood by the open hatchway of the scout, looking toward the town. Gant and Kerry joined him.

A small caravan proceeded along the west road toward the ship. In the lead and dominating the procession was a horselike creature, tall with a bay coat that glistened in the late morning sun. No broad-chested draft animal, this creature was light, lithe, an animal made for running; its long tail seemed unnatural as it nearly swept the dust. On the plains its length would stretch and flow as the animal's stride opened to a ranging gallop.

At his side strode two men, the Deputy Councilor, looking not all that well, and Hargon Mize, the town's leading scholar. A motley group of men straggled behind at a respectful, or cowed, distance.

"That creature won't make it up our ramp," Kerry said. "Let's go out to meet him."

The meadow between road and ship made a neutral and fitting meeting place, home at various times to man and horse. Flies hummed and all other life drowsed in the morning sun.

The lead party from the town halted a half dozen paces from the three Terrans.

"This is the king of this territory's horse folk," Hargon Mize said quietly. There was no need for volume in the meadow's stillness. "He is not certain how precisely some of you can read his projected thoughts, or whether some of you can do so at all. Hence my role. Except as when my opinion is openly sought, I shall now speak his mind."

Gant nodded. Mize moved to stand at the chest of the horse creature, whose eyes surveyed them from above the townsman's own.

"We extend the hospitality of the plains as, no doubt, these men have extended that of their town."

Kerry glanced at Gant. Was this diplomacy or irony? If the latter, Mize was indeed an interpreter supreme, conveying nuance as well as words.

"Thank you," Gant responded. "We have learned from Hargon Mize and others of this town. We hope to learn from you. And perhaps reciprocate."

"One can hope. But I suspect that what you can teach, we would not learn. Nor would we have men here learn it again."

"Technology?" Gant asked. "Technology can save lives. Your people's as well."

"No doubt. But we have long renounced it for the greater good. I doubt if you have any more winning arguments to advance than the men of this world. At any rate, that is not the issue."

"What is, then?" Kerry asked.

"The townsmen of Blye—some of them—are trying to arrange a confrontation wherein I must kill you, or you me."

Gant steeled himself to a steady gaze. He would have liked some input from an experienced hand—like Commander De Silva, who stood behind him out of his line of sight—but was reluctant to back off his lead role. "This is beyond me," he said finally. "We have no wish to kill you. What is your reason?"

"I have no wish, but I do have a reason. These men—again, some of them; not Hargon Mize, for one—would inveigle or coerce technology from you. They may, and likely will, offer to share the planet and their skills in return for freeing men from our yoke. As they see it. I would be wary of such a partnership. The men of this world have greater mental powers than do you, and these are not necessarily true goods of trade. Technology is easier learned—or relearned—than are psi powers and manipulation."

"Yet you live in peace with men," Kerry observed.

"Thousands of years have not fully consolidated that peace, as we are now learning. Some men still seek what they consider freedom. Such men care little for ours."

Both parties stood a moment in silence.

Gant looked again toward Mize and addressed him. "May I solicit your opinion, Hargon, as a man not of the faction that the horse folk fear. How do you view this?"

Mize's gaze sharpened from its inward focus.

"The Horse King is right in many regards, Dr.

Gant. The balance on our world has been struck at a cost. Nature has given the horse folk the only effective means of neutralizing our toolmaking capacity. We had to give it up as the price for peace, and I, for one, do so willingly. Those who do not have been forced to.''

"How?" Kerry asked.

"Some of the horse folk can kill. It is a psi power. The horse folk make them their war commanders, to be obeyed in all times of crisis. In a sense, their kings. We lack this capacity. The battle of our Grasslands War was our technological weaponry against their mind powers. Now some of us wish to reopen the fight with a new weapon. You.''

"I doubt that we'd be so drawn in," Gant said. Kerry thought of some of the colonizing advocates at home and wondered.

"The problem is your capacities and lack of them," Mize continued in the altered tone and inward concentration that denominated the Horse King. "You have the technology, yet you lack a developed telepathic capacity. For the most part. Now some of these men doubt whether you have neural receptors that I can reach. If not, you are a potential lethal weapon in their hands. Our common problem is to have you convincingly renounce ambitions on this world and leave, or have me kill you as a demonstration. If I cannot, it will inflame this world of men. I fear another Grasslands War.''

"Can you kill us?" Kerry asked quietly.

"I do not know. I would rather not try. For better or worse, you show a certain psi receptivity. Dr. Gant has a psi shield. Of sorts. But I would prefer not to think in these terms. It is up to us all to search, rather, for a way out of this dilemma, or the resolution will be forced on us."

Gant looked about him. "I suggest that we think on this. Hasty answers are not the solution. May we resume this talk later?"

The Horse King switched his tail.

"Sunset," Mize said.

The Horse King turned and departed, not back the road toward Blye but across the meadow, loping freely in the interplay of power and beauty that Kerry had earlier imagined. His stride lengthened as he disappeared in a copse of broad-leafed greenery at the meadow's end.

I was the one who saw the way out of it. I had been probing lightly throughout our morning meeting and had been thinking ever since. Sometimes on the run, when thoughts flow most freely.

"Let me take Kerry Burns. She shows the most receptivity. Perhaps we can find a way to reach each other so that all can see that there is more hope in communicating than in killing."

"Where will you take me?" Kerry asked.

"To my psi herd, where those of us who are most skilled can bring these talents to bear."

"I don't know, Kerry," Gant said, sensing the loss of control. I made sure he also sensed the potential loss of his life, and imminently. "What do you want to do?"

The woman looked me head-on, though it was Mize who had spoken throughout. In this way lay our only chance for success. I could only hope that she saw it.

"I'll go," she said.

There is not much to relate of our journey across the western grasslands to the lands of the psi herd by the river. Nothing eventful occurred, and that was the intent. We skirted all human habitations, all roads, and traveled cross-country. We traveled fast.

And yet *things* happened. Not the kind that the eye glimpses nor the sort that quicken the blood or bring the iron tang to the nostril. Rather the thing that the inner self perceives.

I had known before we left that she was reachable. Else why make the journey? What we needed was precisely the lack of external distraction that would hinder the learning. I had to learn how to reach along those strange-yet-not-so-strange neurons, how to breach those alien synapses, how to reach her receptors. She had them, yes—but less developed and subtly different from those I was used to.

She had to learn as well. Things that words could not teach. There were promising signs. The way that she rode, for instance. She sat on my back as though born there, but neither as a rider of command nor a burden to be borne. She made me neither a dray animal nor a thing to be feared. She did her part to make us symbiotic and more—a thing greater together than our sum apart.

No human had ever ridden a Grasslands King. None did now. We rode together.

Toward the end we could communicate mood. I had no trouble reading hers and had sometime since been able to grasp her thoughts. I could impress feelings of alert, danger, and even beauty. Sometimes they were overlaid, one on the other.

The time came when we had to ford the canyon river. We made the crossing below the great cataract, where the river plunges over and down granitic cliffs to spend itself in the Pool of Deeps. I could swim that, and as I did I focused on the power of the cataract, the spume caught in sunlight, the whiteness of the impact water, and the cool green beneath. The woman responded with a squeeze of her legs about my flanks as I breasted the current.

''Are you doing that?'' She had no need to ask, for she knew the answer.

When we reached the psi herd we were friends.

*   *   *

I lost her there, for the moment. It was but a moment, for we could linger but a few days, and I would have her back—again to lose her, for her ship would leave.

The herd did for her what I could not do. They marshaled great forces of community, of numbers, of varied talents. They forced the synapses, melded new passageways. Others had made a start here, we soon learned, allowing her to develop her capabilities at her own rate. This was a luxury we could not afford. Our psi talents led her through the act of communicating, time after time, till the patterns were set for making the mind link with our kind. They held her tenderly and firmly, as a mare might nuzzle a newborn foal to its feet and urge it to its first steps.

On the way back our minds could meet.

It will not be easy for you, I told her. *You know that. The ability to scan and probe where others cannot will terrify even some of an enlightened bent.*

But not all of us, she responded. *I can teach some of us who favor your views, as do I.*

We'll need you as an advocate and an emissary. And as a deterrent to thoughts of colonization. You know that. The alternative is another war.

She paused and surveyed the prairie, our domain, sighting across the windswept meadowland from the vantage of my back—from higher than I could see. Perhaps in other ways as well.

Can I turn those of different views—Gant and those behind him?

She expected no answer. Time alone would furnish it. We hoped she could. Yet her pilgrimage held another purpose which we could not disclose to her: increased knowledge of her kind's mental passageways, triplevers, essence. I—we—could manipulate now with a sureness that would have been guesswork before.

It was a power and a deviousness that I expected to use. The friendship of men and its hope had never been safeguard enough.

The day dawned brightly, burning off the early fog and clearing the dew off grass and cobwebs in quick time. A bright day, indeed. All the factions of this powerplay could regard it as a good augury. I did not scorn the potency of a good omen, but tempered my optimism with the thought that a bright dawning seemed a good sign to all but the blind.

The men of Blye were in good spirits. They escorted me to the meadow along a path now getting worn indeed. We were as gladiators approaching a stadium (we have that legacy, too), united in purpose yet soon to contest. The Deputy Councilor, newly elevated to Prime, walked beside me. It was not in his nature to stride. True, he held the office, but he was ineffectual—the eternal deputy. I recognized several of those nominally beneath him, wearing cloth of coarser weave and no baubles of office, who made up the nobler metals of this human amalgam.

The dust rose from my hooves and hung in the still air, drifting as the vagaries of the smallest breezes took it. Several of the councilors coughed as we neared the ship; not all, I thought, from the dust.

A small scoutship. A prize to be won by the men of this world. A prize we could win only by its exile or destruction. And yet its crew had volition, too; they were players in the game.

Kerry Burns stood in the meadow with Commander Gant. Commander De Silva placed himself behind, more the observer than a participant.

The woman looked ragged. So did Gant. They both looked as if they had been arguing all night and were working to keep it under control. Was this bright day a good omen to them as well?

We stood in silence. Behind me, the Prime Councilor and Mize, the ragged line of townspeople fanned out to make an amphitheater of humanity. Tough-eyed, bold, impetuous—some urged their way to the front ranks for the best view. Others hung back through prudence or fear. No hyperbole was needed to glorify the occasion. In this sleepy meadow a great drama was truly about to be played.

Everyone knew it. By their silence the birds and insects served notice that they had vacated the arena. There were only human rustlings and foot shufflings, throat clearings and coughings. Silence in between.

Hargon Mize strode forth and stood by my flank, his plain garment white in the sun, untrimmed with braid or border. His face, hardly less brown than the staff he leaned on, turned toward the outworlders. He addressed them with my words:

"You have told us that you now return to your base ship, then to your home world. We require—these townsmen no less than I—that you tell us your recommendations to your ruling council regarding our world. Be advised that we desire you not to return."

Gant surveyed the crowd, so far as his field of vision could embrace that arc of humanity. He narrowed his gaze finally to Mize and myself. He spoke mildly, in a voice conciliatory but firm:

"And yet the men of this world urge us to return, to help them. They promise us compensating benefits—development of our latent psi abilities. You've proved the thesis yourself, if I read your experience with Kerry rightly. How can I not present the prospect to my superiors?"

Well done. He had responded without answering the question. His answer seemed that of the sweetest reason, which none could take exception to. I suspected him of worse. Kerry stood whitely beside him, her hands clenching and unclenching slowly. She knew better than to take these words at face value.

I could easily have responded that presenting a

situation was one thing, recommending another—and, again, what would he lobby for? But the drama needed time to build to its best effect. Neither party expected to argue the other to a change of position. All here knew Gant's position to be advocacy of a mission, an embassy, even a colony.

I had Mize continue with rhetorical circumlocution. "We would like you to present the negative prospects as well: the enmity of our people, the prospect of another Grasslands War with you as a party, the very real possibility of your being manipulated out of your technological currency and then discarded by beings—a bit more than men as you view mankind—of far greater psi powers than yours."

"I shall present those possibilities," Gant said shortly, leaving little doubt as to his nonconcern.

That was in far enough, I thought. I had hoped that by now some of the townsmen would have drawn the lines of conflict more clearly. They had set up this confrontation; they would have little regard for Gant's fate. I did not need mental probes to see him through their eyes as deliverer and pawn. These perceptions had been buried deep by minds well disciplined to such strategies.

I could easily read the surface gabble of distraction in the crowd, masking the real intent—the whole overlaid with apprehension and excitement that none attempted to hide.

The Prime Councilor finally stood forth in the

silence that I had let develop. He had his lines but made a bad actor. He delivered them haltingly and without grace. But it would do.

"You promised us that you would work for a cultural exchange. We men of Blye and those beyond urge you to do so. Will you?" Face reddened by his temerity, he stepped back.

Gant held his ground and turned to me. "Apparently I'm damned if I do. Or dead, if I read you rightly."

"No," I said through Mize. "We have decided not to kill you. It would do no good. Your kind would come again, and first blood would be upon us. It would be a bad beginning with worse prospect for a better end. You may recommend what you will."

There was an unruly buzz from the line of humanity arcing behind me and along my flanks. I could feel them press as they lost their fear and closed in. Their thoughts were all too clear and ominously exultant, unmasked now of surface trivia: *He cannot do it!*

The Horse King cannot kill these creatures!
They lack the receptors!
They are ours!

It would be beyond control in but a moment. I dared wait no longer.

In I went, along the pathways we had discovered through teaching Kerry, past Gant's self-vaunted psi shielding. No blind gropings. In I went and made the change.

"Wait!" Gant cracked out. The mob froze. "I *will* recommend. I will recommend that we not return till we attain the maturity to deal with these forces. We shall not break your balance. I shall fight to see that we do not return till both horse folk and men ask it."

The mob was as a roiling ball of humanity hitting the limit of a tether. It stopped short, but the welter and ferment escalated higher. Gant's words had been unlooked for, stiff, clearly not his. The quicker of the men knew wherein lay the change, how greater and more subtle the control than mere killing.

Out of the crowd, his singleness of purpose surfacing above the mass turmoil, strode one of the powers of the town, a man of fierce intent—that of the betrayed. He held a projectile weapon of simple design, spring-loaded but menacing and effective at close range. It was trained on Gant.

Time froze. So did all movement.

There was a sear of mental force and the assassin fell, his face an agony of burnout, the weapon unfired.

The crowd fell back, and once more I felt the awe extended to me, King of Plain and Waste.

All eyes were on me—the Councilor's, those of Hargon Mize, Gant, the townsmen. They looked with fear on Death Dealer.

I knew better.

Two eyes did not look on me, but to a greater

unknown: between stars and across grasslands; within the mind. Those eyes were Kerry Burns'—and they knew horror, power, fear. What it meant to be a dealer of death.

Part V

FULL CYCLE

"Does Gant know that it was you who wiped out his would-be killer?"

Kerry considered, then shook her head. "I don't think so." She stopped and thought again. "I think he was too shaken by the mind control experience, the realization that his shield could be breached and his will taken over. And then that he should be saved from murder by that same subverter of his consciousness. He blames the Horse King."

Damon paced on the mat, his bare toes curling and reaching for grip. "Let's hope he leaves it at that. If he suspects your newfound talents, then you're no safer than I am. He can justify it as defense of the race, perhaps conceal it from himself—but he'll eliminate anyone with power to thwart his ambitions. And he'll have his best shot at it before we reach home.''

Damon looked about the gym and workout room. An unlikely refuge. Still, he was coming to regard it in that light, as Harrod and Kira's library had been his haven in the early days of the *Fairbairn* expedition.

He was on his own now, no Harrod Dan or Kira Sor behind him. No on-ship presence, as when Cortald Dir—stowaway par excellence—had accompanied the *Fairbairn* home as a check on its captain's rage and rancor. Just him and Cortald's shadow.

Perhaps not quite alone. Kerry was an ally with considerable powers now. But those powers were best kept in reserve and concealed.

''Why?'' Kerry asked, picking up on this thread of thought. ''Why don't we eliminate Gant? Immobilize him. Kill him if need be.''

''We could try. I'm not one hundred percent sure we'd succeed. But, in a way, we can't try. I can't, at any rate.''

''He's got to go for his gun first, hey?''

Damon laughed. ''Guess so. I've lost some of my innocence over the years, but not my scruples. I'm not completely sure of Gant—so we don't move. And there's another factor, too. By attacking Gant we bring the Captain in on his side—through sense of duty if not affinity—and that I don't want. At the very worst, the Captain might consider me a sufficient threat to Earth to do anything to keep me off it. Up to suiciding this ship.''

Kerry was doing her pacing act now, seething emotion radiating from her in quantum waves. ''So we do nothing?''

''We cover our asses, bide our time—and make love.''

She grinned. ''Damon Hart's Three Point Program. I like some parts more than others.'' She pushed up against him and reached for his belt buckle. ''For the moment let's forget about covering our asses. Quite the contrary.''

Library. Gym. Stateroom. Wardroom.

Sound mind, sound body, a place to warehouse them and one to stoke them.

And that's shipboard life when you're out of a job.

Damon recalled his watchkeeping turns on the bridge. A little nostalgia there, if a bit forced. That had been pretty boring, too. But it had been his world, with him an active participant in it, with at least some element of prospective danger, the need for alertness.

Gant was supplying that now.

No question about it, you could spend more time thinking and reading than making love. That meant more time at the library than at the gym. The gym was certainly suitable for more conventional forms of workout, but Gant seemed to think so also and was often there seeking judo partners. Damon hoped Gant would work through his frustrations and aggressions there, but not on him, not even in his presence.

The library was a place of no strife and quieter stimulations. Damon could read there or talk about literary styles or whatever with the yeoman. With Vijay, too. Vijay seldom intruded into dangerous or personal waters.

Only once.

"We shall be home in a few days," Vijay observed in his soft and courteous voice. They sat in armchairs, side by side in a corner recess of the library, a small end table between them. Produce a manservant with a brandy decanter on a silver salver and you'd have a men's club scene of nineteenth-century England. Vijay's accent, if not his coloration, was right in character. "What are your plans once we arrive?" He smiled shyly. "If I may ask."

"To give mankind a boot up the evolutionary ladder, away from his dead-end role as a territorially defensive squabbler. Away from fighting over material resources. There'll never be enough for mankind's expanding wants. They always outpace his needs." Damon paused. "Those are the grander philosophical goals. Specifically, to set up education centers to develop everyone's latent psi abilities. To get them thinking toward a noncorporeal, nonmaterial existence on more than a maybe basis. To *show* them how it can be done. To lead them to it, through it."

"These educational centers—they could become temples. Gautama tried to teach the Way in my world, and the priests made him a god. No matter that he disavowed godhead specifically."

Damon found himself wishing for a brandy. This kind of discussion called for it. Or did it?

"Always a danger, Vijay. But if I can make every man a god, they won't need to make one of me."

Vijay smiled ruefully. "Not every man. Some of us have limited psi abilities, so it seems. I appear to be among them. Still, I hope that you will pay early attention to my part of the world. Your approach would be welcomed there without much preliminary spadework."

Damon nodded. "I shall, Vijay—with you to help, I hope. Rachman Khan as well, if he's still alive and in favor. I hope he is. But it seems to be the western world that needs its direction altered the more. There's the danger to our world and the other worlds we confront."

"Kerry—she will be your ally in this endeavor?"

"Yes. And I shall need allies. Not disciples or acolytes, but friends, allies, well-wishers. And well-doers."

"You are correct, Damon. As for myself, I am an apolitical scholar and not at all a man of action. But though others may see this development in political terms—and it does have that side—I, too, share your overview of an evolutionary philosophical phenomenon. So consider me your philosophical ally, if there is such a thing. And perhaps—if it ever came to it, and it is within my abilities—something more.''

Damon met Vijay's quite steady brown eyes and nodded his thanks.

A sword hung in the air. Not an ornate, ceremonial blade, not one with a chased or gem-encrusted hilt, not one of burnished and flashing steel. A yeoman's sword, honest and fit for workaday tasks.

Damon looked at the scholarly Indian directly.

''Your psi powers are not as underdeveloped as you imagine, Vijay. Or you are *feeling* most strongly. Your projection may be an abstraction, but it is almost palpable.''

Vijay nodded his recognition.

''There's more, Vijay,'' Damon prompted. ''You are not the man to proffer his sword, or even think in such terms, unless there is much more.''

Vijay blinked behind his glasses and paused. He picked his words slowly. ''There is always an obverse, a paradoxical element to a Zen conception. And that is what this is, from another land than mine—if Zen allows the conception of *another* land. But I do not mean to split philosophic hairs. The totality of the conception is a poem, though also not mine:

> *"When you meet a master swordsman,*
> *show him your sword.*
> *When you meet a man who is not a poet,*
> *do not show him your poem."*

Damon listened in silence and offered no response.
Vijay inclined his head approvingly. "You have
become a master swordsman, Damon. Or so I deem.
The more so, as you will not willingly unsheath your
sword first, even in self-preservation. I was not sure I
had a sword, nor that I wanted one. But I find I did
have one of a sort—a metaphorical sword, as the one
in those lines; perhaps my very Zen—and I showed
you mine."

"There's still more," Damon said quietly. "Why
did you show it to me?"

"You showed me your poem. Your vision. Your
dream," Vijay said. "I am not a Zen master such as
Rinzai, the man who had that thought a millennium
ago and more. But I shall hazard for him the Zen
extension of those lines. You *are* your poem, your
vision, your dream. And in that conception lies a
danger."

Damon raised an eyebrow.

"Because you *are* your poem, you wear it, show it
to others," Vijay went on. "Even those who are not
poets. But that does not mean that they cannot understand your vision. They understand it too well. It
may yet be everyman's dream, but it is not now.

Some men must be deterred. So that you need not use it, you must show them your sword."

Damon shook his head in negation.

"Possibly I have, Vijay. And probably mistakenly. They already have the power to act before I unsheath."

It was more than a dialogue. In some ways, less. A colloquy? Though only one mind was actually there, alive in the common sense, yet . . . there were other senses to be considered. And there was contact on more levels than two real and sentient, but limited, minds usually achieve. Throughout, Damon was acutely aware that what he was seeing and interacting with was only one vestigial part of that complex entity called Cortald Dir. And a simulated part. Cortald had been on the verge of going beyond concerns of temporal nature, much less those of petty politics. This program was a serious swan song with a touch of Lydian raspberry. Nonetheless . . .

DAMON HART: *Has Dr. Gant attempted a dialogue with you, Cortald?*

CORTALD DIR: *Yes, he has. "Attempted" is a good word for it.*

DAMON HART: *I can imagine. What were the problems?*

CORTALD DIR: *He had trouble sticking to dealing with me as I am. There were long silences, which seemed to discomfit him. He kept forgetting that, while I could discourse at length, even ramble, I had to be asked first, that each response of his must end in a question, or at least in some uncompleted thread of thought that I could pick up on, or challenge. Unless, of course, he could achieve more than a simple verbal linkage.*

DAMON HART: *He can't, not without a physical hookup. And he won't do that. What else did he ask about?*

CORTALD DIR: *You, mostly. Whether you were dangerous to Earth. Whether I was dangerous to Earth.*

DAMON HART: *And you answered?*

CORTALD DIR: *Not by my standards. Which, I pointed out, definitionally shaped the parameters of my response.*

DAMON HART: *How did he take that?*

CORTALD DIR: *Called me worse than a Greek oracle. I did not take that as an insult. Again, he seemed to expect a response to what he considered a provocative remark, forgetting the essence of* what *he was addressing.*

DAMON HART: *You gave him silence, then?*

CORTALD DIR: *Yes.*

DAMON HART: *What was his response to your lack of one?*

CORTALD DIR: *Irritation. Finally, a sense of his own foolishness.*

DAMON HART: *What else did he ask?*

CORTALD DIR: *He asked what you and I discussed. I*

informed him that I wouldn't respond—the program that encapsulated my judgment wouldn't let me.

DAMON HART: *What then?*

CORTALD DIR: *He asked whether I would relay the substance of our dialogue to you, should you ask.*

DAMON HART: *And you said?*

CORTALD DIR: *That I would, Damon. And I did add, because it was an implicit part of his question, that it was because the program that encapsulated my judgment mandated that I so inform you.*

DAMON HART: *I'll wager that that was close to the end of the discussion. Right?*

CORTALD DIR: *Right. I'd say that Dr. Gant took a perverse pleasure in terminating the dialogue. I'd guess that he preferred to fancy that he was cutting off a real person.*

DAMON HART: *Do I have to ask you, Cortald, if your judgment considers Malcolm Gant dangerous to Earth? Or to me? By your standards, of course.*

CORTALD DIR: *No, Damon. You don't have to ask.*

Damon was half dozing, half musing. No sound in his compartment, no music. Perhaps a faint mechanical hum from the air exchanger. Darkness.

Something less. Or more. A sound, or lack of it. Something different. Damon tried to sit up in his bunk. He couldn't: motor paralysis. The first tendrils of alarm, themselves dampened, raced to his consciousness. Time was fractions of a second, the space between heartbeats. No heartbeat. His autonomic nervous system was also shutting down.

Out-of-body. Fast. Or never.

Damon cut loose, wrenchingly, painfully. An abandon-ship drill he had hoped never to use. The perception of *human* as linked to the body was going forever. Behind him the paralytic death nipped at the heels of his psyche.

Adrift. Out-of-body and truly alone. Tossed overboard and sighting down the wake of his vessel, already distancing itself from his reach, never to return.

And no handy receptacle. Damon knew that he could last a very finite time without a matrix to lend order to his inchoate form. But he could spare long enough to fill the room with his receptors, surround and survey his body: cooling, still on the bunk built into the bulkhead. Darkness was no problem. Sound was the key—the smallest hiss of a gas being introduced into the stateroom from some nozzled hidden recess. Nerve gas, almost certainly.

No need for deep theorizing toward tracking down the perpetrator. Damon knew already. Nor would Gant prove shy once Damon's body was demonstrably and palpably cold.

Out and through the ship. Physical barriers were nothing now, steel bulkheads the sheerest gauze. Through the passageways, around and through all material obstacles—ship's crew included. Shortcutting familiar routes, melting between deck levels, down and aft to Secondary Conn.

The same sleepy watch conditions held sway in Secondary Conn. Night and day cycles were meaningless, activity nil at all times. A bored lieutenant jg slouched in his chair wondering how to avoid entanglements with a girlfriend who had promised to wait for him despite his diplomatic and finally blunt protestations. That was one of his years ago, four or five of hers. Young he was, but cynical enough to hope that humankind's track record of inconstancy when laid out longitudinally on a time axis would work toward his favored solution. *Good God!—Monica would be thirty-two!*

The lieutenant's quartermaster slouched in another chair, figuring that ass was ass and looking forward to acquiring some of any age, soonest.

Cortald Dir's psi terminal stood open, imprinted since Damon's first visit to accept his entrance. Incorporeal, unnoticed by this lethargic watch duo, Damon went into the computer.

Gant could have waited for Damon's body to be discovered by others. Kerry Burns, most likely.

He didn't. Within minutes of clinical death, almost as soon as the air in Hart's compartment had been pumped out and outboard, Gant was in. It was a night cycle and the passageways were virtually empty. Deep night. Only watchkeepers, game players, and other assorted insomniacs manned their stations or were in any form awake.

Gant and two medical corpsmen rolled Damon's inert body onto a motorized trolley, then convoyed it through the ship to sick bay. They brushed past the stares of the curious, wheeled into the medical quarters, and secured the hatches behind them.

Gant looked down at Damon and stood quietly for a moment, then nodded. He beckoned his corpsmen forward. Quickly they stripped Damon down, swabbed the body clean of excrement. They rolled the body to a waiting cryogenic chamber and lifted Damon in.

Gant followed, arms clasped behind him, a triumphant Napoleon and a brooding one as well. He looked at Damon through the transparent panel, noted the refrigerating crystallization of moisture at his lips. He nodded again and strode to his desk, once that of the ship's doctor. Like Commander De Silva of Alien Contact, the ship's doctor had been dispossessed of his power base and even his base territory. Sick bay was Gant's and so was the medical officer's desk. Gant seated himself, taking a moment or two to make himself suitably comfortable. He punched alive the communications unit.

The bridge messenger answered briskly, "Bridge, Aye."

"Commander Gant here. I'm in sick bay. Tell the OOD I'd like a word with him."

The OOD's face filled the screen, interested in this

break in routine. An open face, freckled and full-cheeked. "Commander," he acknowledged noncommittally.

"Is the Captain awake, Lieutenant?"

"No sir. He turned in three hours ago as I was coming on. No word from him since."

"Please wake him, Lieutenant. Inform him that I'd like to speak to him."

The OOD looked pointedly at the bridge chronometer, in Gant's view. "My orders—the bridge standing orders—are not to wake the Captain short of an emergency situation. Is this an emergency that I should know about?"

Gant was relaxed and in control, a successful mission against a far more potent adversary than the OOD under his belt. He accepted with amusement the feistiness of the lieutenant and this exercise of his four-hour term of power to protect the Captain.

"Mr. Hart is dead."

The OOD froze momentarily.

"No danger to the ship or personnel," Gant added after a moment.

"Stand by, Commander. I'll wake the Captain."

Gant utilized the confusion and the time lag to ease back comfortably in his chair. He looked benignly around him at sick bay, his fiefdom. A modest fiefdom. But changes were in the wind.

The screen split and the Captain's face appeared, sharing the presentation with a wide-angle view of the bridge, all watchkeepers going about make-work tasks so as to appear disinterested from the proceedings while picking up as much of them as they could. The Captain had worked the focus so that his face filled his segment, affording no view of disarrayed nightclothes or underwear to undercut his image. His first words were to order the OOD back to normal deck routine, to dismiss him and the bridge from the comm circuit. The OOD blanked out, leaving the Captain's face to fill the entire screen.

"What happened?" he asked tersely.

"Mr. Hart is dead, gassed in his quarters at my orders. His body is here at sick bay and frozen. It will be autopsied on Earth and the brain, particularly, studied."

The Captain looked evenly ahead, not blinking. "My orders to both of you were to abstain from acts of violence against each other. In that domain my orders carry precedence, no matter your position elsewhere. If murder weren't crime enough, you've disobeyed the orders of the Captain of this ship. Explain yourself."

"Your orders were not to abstain from violence," Gant said equably, leaning deliberately back and propping a knee against the desk. "They were to commit no action that would provoke a fight endangering the ship. I did not endanger the ship, nor can anyone make a case that I did. I did kill Mr. Hart and am quite ready to answer for it before a general court-martial.'' Gant abandoned his relaxed pose and leaned forward intently. ''Or *higher* authority. It is their province to judge and perhaps punish. Your power in capital matters is to—at most—restrain. And, I assure you, I am going nowhere.''

The Captain seemed in no way daunted by this sophistic exercise. He matched Gant stare for challenging stare.

''You *are* going somewhere, short-term. Your movements or lack of them, as you point out, are my domain. Report to my quarters immediately.''

Gant touched his forehead in grave salute, though he wore no hat. ''Aye, aye, sir,'' he said, enjoying the anachronistic words as they rolled off his tongue.

Grass-green fields, hilly and rolling. Fences of white-painted wood. Horses grazing unconcernedly, tails flicking to discourage flies.

Kerry had two apples in her bikepack. Just the thing to complete the idyll—whickering horses to pick them daintily from her hand, tails swishing in equine satisfaction.

Kerry had no intention of calling those horses to her or feeding apples to them should they unaccountably come. She intended to eat the apples.

The apples were incidental, in any case. They were the clincher to winning permission to squat in a Miwok Indian lodge and fantasize about aborigines and becoming an anthropologist, a word whose meaning the twelve-year-old Kerry Burns had recently learned.

Kerry's parents would never have given permission for that, for letting her take her bike on the skimmerway from the Olema campground where the family was roughing it in electrically hooked-up rusticity, to grub in real mud and dust. True, the mud was dried mud at this time of year. And one could make a telling argument on the grounds of cultural education and enrichment. But that was not Kerry's way, nor, in fact, the best way to the desired end.

Kerry Burns had a big edge in this manipulation. She already knew the difference between sentiment and true feeling, though her parents didn't. Further, Kerry had learned the strength of appealing to the image of herself in a sentimental setting as a means of getting what she wanted.

"Mom, Dad—can I bicycle back to the park? To see the horses?"

"Why do you want to do that, Kerry?" her father had asked absently from before the sports simulator. "You saw the horses when we walked the Earthquake Trail. Wasn't it more interesting seeing the fault line and learning about tectonic plates? And seeing where that cow supposedly fell in when the ground split? Besides, you can see horses at home."

"Not Morgan horses, Daddy. This is almost the only place they have them anymore. And we only saw them from far off."

Kerry's father looked over her to Kerry's mother, who was making an afternoon project of preparing a country dinner. Whatever that was. She was bored stiff.

"They were beautiful, Daddy, the way they ran. I'd like to feed them some apples."

"Those teeth can bite, you know," her father had said, and Kerry knew that she had won.

Miwok Indians and Morgan horses. An unlikely combination. Cheyenne and horses, galloping over a windswept prairie, that was more like it. The Miwoks were coastal Indians, had lived in the California woods, fished in local bays and mud flats, and had probably seen horses only briefly before the Spaniards—who had brought them to their proximity—had also conveyed the diseases that killed off the Miwoks.

Still, for a century now, standing side by side at the Point Reyes National Seashore were a Morgan horse ranch and a rude and reconstructed Miwok village. An unlikely juxtaposition—two relics of different eras—but there and abutting each other.

Kerry leaned her bike against an acacia sapling where the road ended, drew her chainlock around it and secured it. Out of reach of horses' teeth from the other side of the fence. The handlebars were salty and just might appeal as much as an apple. She was no expert on the subject and didn't care about finding out.

She took a moment to study the horses, sturdie

than Arabians but graceful in their way. She had to be able to describe them, their movements, the bucolic setting. It was a pleasant duty. Kerry could appreciate the beauty here, but that still was not the main object.

Image of Horse King overlaying the scene. Grace and something more. Perception. Piercing intelligence. Grasslands as domain, not enclosure. Freedom.

Kerry banished this intrusive image, grudgingly. A good vision, but not this one.

She began walking along the rutted path by the fence, leaving the horses behind finally, and working through the greenery of a wooded copse. Bay and eucalyptus, mainly. Long strips of eucalyptus bark hung in strips from self-denuding trunks. A pungency filled the air, bracing and almost medicinal. Perhaps medications had been derived from this grove centuries ago.

A clearing, then—and the village. Twig and mud huts, constantly eroding or being washed away by winter rains as in olden days, now perpetually being built up by park rangers and visitors under their supervision. Kerry had wanted to take a turn in this ongoing project. Her parents had no interest in more than a cursory examination of the village and had pulled her away to tramp the Earthquake Trail.

There was no one here now.

The buildings were new, but the site was real. Real artifacts had come from a real midden here.

Indians had walked and worked and reproduced here long before there were cows around to fall in earthquake fissures. If any ever had.

Kerry walked the paths between the rude huts and lean-tos. Under one overhang she stopped to study the flint and wooden tools, their purpose, workmanship, ornamentation. Pots, baskets, and half-finished garments helped her reconstruct the work process.

Finally the central lodge, which her parents had dragged her by. She had wanted to go in. Its entrance had beckoned like a Delphic cave. Partly sunk beneath ground level, the lodge nonetheless loomed as the most imposing structure in the village. Kerry stooped to manage the igloolike entrance tunnel of mud topped with twigs. At the end of a ten-foot passage the room opened out to a wide circle. The dirt was well trodden. Still, her passage had stirred up dust. Kerry walked around the central fire pit, deliberately kicking up more of it. The sun slanted in shafts down the open vent hole in the roof. It caught the whirling cloud of dust, turned it into columns of smoke. The closest thing to smoke that Kerry could manage.

Kerry squatted by the fire pit and focused on the dust/fire in a single-minded concentration of self-hypnosis. She saw the circle completed by naked, sweating bodies. Male, of course. Eyes gleamed whitely; teeth as well. Some tossed gambling stones idly; a few with fervor as others watched, grunted.

whooped. Others squatted motionlessly, as she did now, and sought in the smoke their visions as she searched in this time removed. Time passed and had no meaning.

Kerry.

Kerry shifted in her bed, clutching the bedclothes. She reached for Damon and reached to hold on to that long gone quest.

Kerry.

It couldn't be done. Too much to hold.

Kerry.

Kerry felt the brush of his mind like a warm and loving hand, not on any one part of her body but on all of it and her inner self as well. She rolled over, pulling her legs up as if to entwine them about his thighs. Sleepily she murmured his name.

Damon took it slowly, bringing her awake in delicate stages. He touched and caressed with his mind till she was awake enough to know it and to ask him to come to her.

I can't, Kerry. Except like this.

Why? The first intimations of alarm were intruding, bringing her to fuller consciousness.

Gant's had me killed. My body, anyway. Nerve gassed in my bed.

Kerry sat bolt upright and turned on the light, looking about her as if willing his physical presence.

I'm out-of-body now. Can't keep that up too long, though I'm working on it.

Where else then?

The computer. No constraints, like the city or the other worlds; no company either. It's a spartan base, but it'll sustain me. Thanks to Cortald Dir it even has a few custom touches its Terran designers never dreamed of. So I'll survive, and not all that badly.

Damon—stop babbling on so bravely! Can't we do anything?

Not to get my body back. Yes, to safeguarding yours.

And to do in Mac Gant!

Yes to that, too. I can justify that now—even to myself. He's a megalomaniac and a continuing danger. To you in particular and to any progress that erodes his power base.

How?

Get to the Captain. Get him to release Gant from confinement to quarters. I want you to do it—I don't want him or Mac knowing I'm sentient. Alive.

How can I do that?

I think you can be direct. Almost direct. Without saying it outright, let the Captain know that Gant can still manipulate dangerously from his stateroom, but that you can guarantee to stop him in a way that won't embarrass him if you can get at Gant openly during shipboard routine. You can hint broadly. I don't think the Captain will press you for details. He

*wants the same thing we do—if it can be managed
without him and without a mess.*

Can we do it?

*I can do it. You can, too. You learned that from
the Horse King. I regret that we have to.*

*I don't. I'm an unreconstructed pre-Orestes Greek.
Put me with the Furies. I want Mac Gant dead!*

What Kerry needed—and was not going to get—
was a beach for walking. Striding. A low-tide beach
with wet and hard-packed sand at the water level,
long and stretching, without coves or promontories to
slow or halt a relentless stride. Kerry did not want to
slog her way over the drag of shifting dunes or
scramble over rock outcroppings that met the sea at
the tideline. She wanted pace and an unchanging
seascape, and a background rumble and crash to still
voices. She wanted no humans around to give voice
to anything. The voices in her head were quite enough.

There were no breakers or lowering skies, no shore-
birds or driftwood. Not on a ship. Not on this type of
a ship. She'd settle for an oceangoing vessel with an
outside deck and a high wind and no one to intrude
on her attempt at solitude.

This ship held no outside deck and no sea, and
every walk was along peopled corridors that led to a
utilitarian somewhere. You could not trace an endless
perimeter and you could not avoid purposeful shipboard personnel.

You couldn't be alone.

People spoke to Kerry. They treated her like a widow.

The ones who spoke least comforted her best. Vijay came up to her, took both hands and held them, imparting a firm and dry pressure. He met her eyes directly and held the gaze a moment. He nodded, released one hand and clasped the other with both of his, stepped back and turned away.

Roger Chabron came up and told her that he was at her disposal "in any way you would find comforting." She came close to kneeing him in the groin.

Mac Gant kept out of her way. It was a large ship, and their spheres of activity had diverged. Kerry could and did avoid the wardroom, not only to keep away from Gant but all those less sinister of the ship's officers as well, the semisympathetic and the gawking curious. There was her stateroom, but she felt even less alone in its cramped confines. Voices and memories intruded and wouldn't be banished. They stayed in the room—also confined by its bulkheads, bouncing back off them till she covered her eyes and ears with her hands. Or got up and fled.

There was the gym. Working out—judo, particularly—was the closest thing she could manage to that unattainable beach walk. Her workout partners were immersed in the judo and approached her as an opponent/player, not an object of sympathy or curiosity. But, then, there was Gant. It had been only a couple of days, and he had not been at the gym when Kerry worked out.

Gant. She ought to work quickly, before Gant had second thoughts about her. Apparently he did not consider her a present danger, or he would have had her killed simultaneously with Damon. Kerry did not doubt that he had the lethal mechanical means, whether in her stateroom or elsewhere. Perhaps he hadn't wanted to compound the crime, figuring that a multiplicity of deaths might be harder to justify on Earth. That could change.

Damon had suggested that she play up to Gant. Stroke his vanity, his power drive. He would likely be pleased by a limited show of respect bordering on fear. Kerry wasn't good at playacting. She was ready to act in earnest, and fast.

Gant looked about him, then strode forward boldly and forthrightly, the gym and workout room very much a microcosm of the ship. And soon, more.

His *gi* was freshly laundered and had no smell of sweat to it. And why should it? As yet no exercise, certainly no apprehension. Let others fear and mistrust. Perhaps even hate. Machiavelli had shown that to be no drawback to the exercise of power.

Heady thoughts, and perhaps a bit overstated, in this context of ship's crew out for a workout. A more tolerant, lenient viewpoint was likely in order when dealing with such as these. A bit of noblesse oblige.

Gant ambled over to Matthews, a burly electronics technician, second class. Matthews was finishing his *ukemi*, coming off a warming-up series of forward rolls. He wore a brown belt, second degree; Gant had enjoyed pitting his skills in past sessions against the heavier man's brawny strength. An enlisted man— though well advanced in a technical specialty—he was just the one to serve as an example of Gant's accessibility to the common folk.

"A little *uchikomi*, Harve?" Gant asked jovially, addressing Matthews familiarly. "Want to work on your *seoi nage*? You almost got me with that last time."

Matthews looked at Gant coolly. He, at least, showed no apprehension. "Thanks, no, Commander. I'm still not loosened up. I'll work on my falls and rolls a bit longer."

Matthews turned away abruptly but unhurriedly and started another series of rolls, his outstretched arm hitting the mat with resounding slaps. Slaps in the face to Gant. He should have probed before approaching Matthews, read the hostility before being confronted with it overtly. So much for abstaining from the use of a power on lesser men.

A little less confidently Gant began a patrol of the mat area. Most of the *judokas* kept out of his way, some pressing their backs into the wall to do so. Gant found that perversely pleasing.

Kerry Burns stood her ground, regarding Gant from

over the shoulder of her workout partner, a slightly built Japanese from Communications. No probe attempts by Gant here; she'd pick up on that. As Gant approached, Kerry was finishing a series of step-in repetitions—*hane goshi*, a throw requiring fine timing.

"You might try getting in a bit closer, Kerry, before you start the leg move," Gant tossed out offhandedly as he swung by.

"It's tough against a strong man," Kerry said between breaths. Her brow was beaded with perspiration. "Yosh is cooperating now, but in *randori* he usually straight-arms me."

Gant was past Kerry now and had to make an effort to avoid stopping short. Kerry already had a workout partner and had shown no previous receptivity to him at the workout room.

"Let me show you," he said, and turned for permission to the Japanese, who bowed deferentially to his rank and backed off. Gant reached for Kerry's sleeve with his left hand, her lapel with his right. "In *randori*, try to wait till your opponent is committed to coming in before you pivot. You'll get him coming in close to you of his own accord. If he tries to straight-arm you, you can shift grip inside his arm like this. If his arms end up outside, he's got to bend them."

Kerry cocked her head attentively. "May I try a few?"

"Sure. Go ahead."

Kerry's aroma was an intoxicating mixture of skin-warmed body scent and sweat. Gant found it aphrodisiac. To his surprise he was perspiring also. Would Kerry find that stimulating? Intriguing thought!

Kerry was doing step-ins. Gant had never worked with her. She pivoted fast and had a good wrist snap, making up in quickness and concealment of her move what she lacked in strength. In—out. In—out.

"You're getting it. Try it now with me straight-arming you."

Kerry's copper hair had a sun-warmed smell, though they were light years from the nearest sun. Or was he romanticizing wildly?

"Lots better."

"But would it work in *randori*, when you're trying to throw me?"

"We could try," Gant suggested, ready to press any advantage. *Randori*—open competition. With Hart gone, was Kerry ready to transfer allegiance, perhaps testing through judo combat for a man of suitable strength?

"But you know what throw I'm working on."

"Doesn't matter," Gant said. "Nagano is a *seoi nage* man—everyone knows it. He picks up Olympic gold anyway, because he's so good at it. Even his setup throws are good. I don't know yours; you might get me on one."

"Let me catch my breath a moment." Kerry re leased her handgrip and backed off, wiping her brow and adjusting her *gi,* which had fallen open. Unlike most women, she wore no shirt under the jacket.

Gant flushed and reached down to his own belt—a black one, *Nidan*—and centered the knot. They walked together to the center of the mat as others moved out of their way.

Gant bowed to Kerry, she to him. They gripped each other's *gi*s and Gant nodded. They started a circle to the left. Gant tried an ankle block and Kerry skipped over it, countering with a thigh sweep, but from too far out. Exploratory stuff. They circled again, Gant laying back, making no attempt to probe and patiently waiting to counter. Gant tuned to receptivity mode, but Kerry was putting out nothing at all, forcing Gant to read her intentions through hand and body movement. She *was* good, telegraphing nothing.

Here she came, in for her hip throw—a good tactic against a taller opponent. Probably *hane goshi* or *seoi nage*. Gant started to bend his knees to provide the block of a lower profile.

Fake—a setup! Not a setup to *hane goshi,* but *hane goshi* as the setup! Kerry was reversing her pivot, hooking her right leg behind his left knee and driving her left shoulder into his left, forcing him back to that corner. She had him off-balance, on one leg, and she was hopping now, driving him back. His weight was completely off his right leg, and she was hooking his left out from under him.

Gant was down on his back—thrown. *Ouchi gari.*

Not the cleanest, most elegant of throws—probably not the full point of an *ippon*. And Kerry knew this. She had dropped to the mat with him, her right arm tucked under his neck in a quick *kesa gatame*. Fast! She was grabbing the wrist of her encircling right arm with her left hand and going for a choke, burying her head against his cheek and chin for leverage. Suddenly the aroma of her hair and body was less intoxicating than he had hoped.

Gant quickly bridged and rolled. It worked. Once he got her over the balance point he let his greater weight do it for him, rolling over till he turned the tables to the same hold on her.

But she had her hands free between his as he tried to tuck his head into hers. Suckered again! As he lowered his head within reach she drove her hands quickly up and along both sides of his neck in a cross-armed hold, each hand grabbing his loose *gi* at the neck. She pulled in and across, rolling her wrists till the bones knifed across his carotid arteries. An effective choke. He had only seconds to break it, counter, or give up. Otherwise he'd be blacking out.

He started to bear out, to break the choke. He couldn't move his arms.

Kerry relaxed the choke but held her position. "You can't move because I've blocked those motor functions. You're a captive audience. Listen up."

Gant tried lifting off her with his legs. Without the use of his arms, locked around Kerry's head but unable either to exert pressure or withdraw, it was just so much useless thrashing.

"You're going to die, Mac—just like Damon. You'll have his chance—he wants it that way. He thinks that if you get out-of-body you'll be free of desire for these murderous intrigues. I rather doubt it."

"Hart's alive?" Gant rasped.

"Out-of-body. And that's your only chance. Listen up, for here it is. You're going to slap the mat and give up, or I'll choke you to blackout. Your choice. Then I step up and away. You'll have a couple of minutes on the mat to recover. You can walk around a bit. I give you a few minutes to get yourself prepared to go out-of-body. Then that body's dead."

"Hart going to kill me?"

"I am—though no one else will realize it. Just like I killed your would-be murderer on the horse folk's world."

"The Horse King . . ."

"Me." Kerry tightened her grip again and rolled her wrists into Gant's arteries. "Now slap—or blackout!"

Gant slapped. Kerry got up slowly and turned her back to Gant.

I can't make it out-of-body, Gant projected from his sitting position, rubbing his neck. He was the center of attention, all too unwelcome now. Even the gymnasts on the horse and rings had stopped their workout to focus on him.

Try.

Gant tried. It was a foredoomed effort, cut by panic and the knowledge that there was no stabilizing matrix to retreat to even if he could cut loose from his flesh. He rose to his feet and started across the mat toward Kerry, his hand out in untypical supplication.

Her back to him, from twenty feet away, Kerry went in. She brushed past his psi shield and burned him out. Gant pitched forward to his knees, dead before his face hit the mat.

Leave-takings. Homecomings. He cut loose the clasp and let them roll opalescently before him, pearls off a string.

Leaving Earth. Crisply uniformed, full of hope, yet youthfully sure that he had purged himself of illusion. A leave-taking full of promise, adventure before him and little to regret.

The night before the *Fairbairn* departed Lydia, leaving him behind. Adventure and promise of a different kind. Also the label of exile, deserter, principled man of action. Pick the label, try it for size.

The night before leaving Lydia, the last union with Kira, Kerry, Maldir, and all the faceted personae they had brought to that congress. Now he lived on as a background reflection to Kira's pairings.

Leaving his body forever. Untimely, traumatic, painful—but simply an advance up the time scale of what must ultimately be.

And now the night before landfall on Earth. Coming home. Not the homecoming of the Damon Hart who once had been. The starched uniform was gone, sweat-soaked before he had reached the base of the gangway those years ago. The illusions and the youthful cynicism were gone, his very body was gone. And what remained? Or had accreted to make up what he now was?

There were leave-takings and homecomings ahead. Perhaps a return to Lydia, perhaps with Kerry. To Kira, to what Kira would become, to the city.

He knew the richness and poetry of the city, but it was an Earthman's word images that shimmered out of blackness.

Keep Ithaka always in your mind.
Arriving there is what you're destined for.
But don't hurry the journey at all.
Better if it lasts for years,
so you're old by the time you reach the island,
wealthy with all you've gained on the way,
not expecting Ithaka to make you rich.

For others as well: coming home. For centuries that blend of intermingled hopes and fears for all sailors, to some the prospects more terrifying than the voyage. Unfaithful lovers, deaths since departure. One newer certainty of this era: faithful or unfaithful, lovers or adversaries—all those who waited would have aged several years to every traveler's one.

Kerry had no close family. The one person who now mattered to her would no longer age physically. Her recent adversary was dead at her hand.

A hell of a way to start a brave new world, she growled.

Regrets?

None.

The crew was disembarking, their families and friends—or no one—awaiting in the arrival hall. Not for Kerry, Vijay, Chabron. For such as these a lengthy debriefing waited. Or, at least, had originally been laid on. Physical examinations, interrogations, deep psi probes (as best the government's talents could muster), sleep and hypnotic delvings. The government had much at stake and knew it: its life versus theirs.

Damon had acted preemptively and quickly. Before decontamination quarantine had been lifted, a part of him was reaching out to the world's power wielders with a brief and forceful message, delivered through their most secure comm lines or directly, inside their heads. With intractable disbelievers he backed up the message with control of bodily functions. This ability to penetrate their sanctums and security was itself the core of the message. Hart was back and alive, close to ubiquitous, able to survey and to act. To tap the world's communications networks and reach the masses anytime he chose. To deal death as he, not Kerry—a calculated misdirection here—had dealt to Gant.

There would be no forced government debriefing under conditions of restraint.

Vijay, Chabron, and Kerry waited out the crew's exodus in the Captain's in-port cabin. A part of Damon waited too, his sentient presence just recently unveiled to Vijay, Chabron, and the Captain. Vijay had taken it with aplomb. Chabron had responded by withdrawal, hardly daring to venture any thought at all in Damon's unseen presence—the legacy of a long line of farmwives' provincial superstitions overriding his scientific veneer. The Captain had nodded briefly in acceptance, then had left the three in favor of supervising the debarkation routine.

The hatch opened. A slightly built man, sinewy and erect, stepped in and faced the group. He secured the hatch behind him while facing forward. No wasted motion and a familiarity with shipboard fittings. The feel of military presence was counterpointed by his plain tunic and the absence of badges, braid, or insignia.

"Rachman Khan Pindharee," he stated from the hatchway. "Welcome back. A *personal* welcome." He nodded to each in turn. "Dr. Chabron. My friend, Chaudhuri. Dr. Burns. And Damon Hart, too?"

Yes, Rachman.

"I had looked forward to shaking your hand, Damon."

And I yours. The mind touch must do for us now.

"A deeper contact, perhaps an intimacy. We'll have time for that, I hope. Perhaps even an occasional game of chess. But you have a whole world to reach and—it seems—to educate. Perhaps to lead."

"Is that the government's position, Colonel Khan?" Kerry asked sharply. "Have they come to acceptance so early?"

"Rachman, please. And yes—they have been brought to it, though there certainly are strong factions and individuals who do not relish such revolutionary changes as Damon's plans portend. They would block such efforts."

"We've seen such actions," Kerry pursued. "That's why Damon is dead, in body at least."

"And we've seen the response in Malcolm Gant's death and in Damon's out-of-body contacts with certain men of power today. As both Damon and I have long known, and he has newly demonstrated, that is the only way to reach such people before they reach you. Unfortunate but true. But please do not consider me in that number or as a spokesman for such leaders. I am not."

Enough, Rachman. And you, too, Kerry. This is a meeting of friends, and I am quite effectively beyond the reach of any enemies, ironically, thanks to thei man, Gant. They are not beyond mine. But Rachman is not here as an emissary or public person. He doesn't have to convey my position to anybody. I can reach anybody, anytime. That's protection for you, and that's power. He paused. *And it can also be friendship.*

Rachman Khan smiled. "You have changed, Damon. And grown. For the moment you are unique on this world, an outsider in the truest sense—the first of us to stand outside the body and still maintain contact with those of us not yet there. An exemplar to many, an insurrectionist and bandit chief to those entrenched." He paused and added wryly, "It is not I, but you, who are Pindharee."

Damon embraced the group and surveyed a far greater domain at the same time: Cortald Dir's world-wide network of computers and psi terminals. Damon's growing ability to live for longer periods out-of-body. His ability to divide his presence and his receptors. Other developments were accreting to his psyche in rapid stages. Was this the end to which he was working? Or did increased awareness bring greater goals?

He reveled in the feeling of freedom as his spirit expanded to fill its new and larger limits. Still, a part of him longed to lie with Kira, with Kerry again—to hold them both in physical closeness. Though they, too—Kira especially—might be growing, in different aspects, away from such desires. And Kerry as well, in time.

Time.

Time enough to find out. To find each other in the City again, if their desires still so commonly melded.

Later.

THE BEST IN SCIENCE FICTION

☐ 53300-3   THE INFINITY LINK by Jeffrey Carver $3.95
  53301-1   Canada $3.95

☐ 53253-8   ENDER'S GAME by Orson Scott Card $3.50
  53254-6   Canada $3.95

☐ 55113-5   SANTIAGO: A MYTH OF THE FAR
          FUTURE by Mike Resnick $3.50
  55133-3   Canada $3.95

☐ 54333-5   CV by Damon Knight $2.95
  54334-3   Canada $3.50

☐ 55625-9   BRIGHTNESS FALLS FROM THE AIR $3.50
  55626-7   by James Tiptree, Jr.   Canada $3.95

☐ 53150-7   THE KUNDALINI EQUATION $3.50
  53151-5   by Steven Barnes   Canada $4.25

☐ 55235-0   THE MEMORY OF WHITENESS $3.50
  55236-9   by Kim Stanley Robinson   Canada $4.50

☐ 53122-1   THE EDGE OF TOMORROW $3.50
  53123-X   by Isaac Asimov   Canada $4.50

☐ 53271-6   UNIVERSE 14 edited by Terry Carr $2.95
  53272-4   Canada $3.50

☐ 53273-2   TERRY CARR'S BEST SCIENCE $3.50
  53274-0   FICTION OF THE YEAR (#14)   Canada $3.95

Buy them at your local bookstore or use this handy coupon:
Clip and mail this page with your order

TOR BOOKS—Reader Service Dept.
49 W. 24 Street, New York, N.Y. 10010

Please send me the book(s) I have checked above. I am enclosing
$_____ (please add $1.00 to cover postage and handling).
Send check or money order only—no cash or C.O.D.'s.

Mr./Mrs./Miss _____

Address _____

City _____ State/Zip _____

Please allow six weeks for delivery. Prices subject to change without
notice.

Ben Bova

☐	53200-7	AS ON A DARKLING PLAIN		$2.95
	53201-5		Canada	$3.50
☐	53217-1	THE ASTRAL MIRROR		$2.95
	53218-X		Canada	$3.50
☐	53212-0	ESCAPE PLUS		$2.95
	53213-9		Canada	$3.50
☐	53221-X	GREMLINS GO HOME		$2.75
	53222-8	(with Gordon R. Dickson)	Canada	$3.25
☐	53215-5	ORION		$3.50
	53216-3		Canada	$3.95
☐	53210-4	OUT OF THE SUN		$2.95
	53211-2		Canada	$3.50
☐	53223-6	PRIVATEERS		$3.50
	53224-4		Canada	$4.50
☐	53208-2	TEST OF FIRE		$2.95
	53209-0		Canada	$3.50

Buy them at your local bookstore or use this handy coupon:
Clip and mail this page with your order

TOR BOOKS—Reader Service Dept.
49 W. 24th Street, 9th Floor, New York, NY 10010

Please send me the book(s) I have checked above. I am enclosing
$_____ (please add $1.00 to cover postage and handling).
Send check or money order only—no cash or C.O.D.'s.

Mr./Mrs./Miss _____
Address _____
City _____ State/Zip _____
Please allow six weeks for delivery. Prices subject to change without
notice.